*"Oh, Paul! ~~Don't leave me~~"* Joy cried,

launching herself at the man inside the patrol car.

Officer Mike Jessup's jaw dropped as he watched Joy Marie Cooper, his daughter's schoolteacher, kiss the breath out of the stranger who had just requested a police escort to his ship. The man looked dazed when Joy let him come up for air.

"Paul, please don't leave me," she repeated brokenly, crocodile tears rolling down her cheeks.

She cast a pitiful glance at the bewildered trooper. "Don't let him do this," she begged. "If not for me..."

Letting the sentence hang on a shuddering breath, Joy cast an audacious wink at Paul.

"...then for the baby...."

Dear Reader,

Favorite author Kasey Michaels starts off the month with another irresistible FABULOUS FATHER in *The Dad Next Door*. Quinn Patrick was enjoying a carefree bachelor life-style until Maddie Pemberton and her son, Dillon, moved next door. And suddenly Quinn was faced with the prospect of a ready-made family!

A BUNDLE OF JOY helps two people find love in *Temporarily Hers* by Susan Meier. Katherine Whitman would do anything to win custody of her nephew, Jason, even marry playboy Alex Cane—temporarily. But soon Katherine found herself wishing their marriage was more than a temporary arrangement....

Favorite author Anne Peters gives us the second installment in her miniseries FIRST COMES MARRIAGE. Joy Cooper needed a *Stand-in Husband* to save her reputation. Who better for the job than Paul Mallik, the stranger she had rescued from the sea? Of course, love was never supposed to enter the picture!

The spirit of the West lives on in Pat Montana's *Storybook Cowboy*. Jo McPherson didn't want to trust Trey Covington, the upstart cowboy who stirred her heart. If she wasn't careful, she might find herself in love with the handsome scoundrel!

This month, we're delighted to present our PREMIERE AUTHOR, Linda Lewis, debuting with a fun-filled, fast-paced love story, *Honeymoon Suite*. And rounding out the month, look for Dani Criss's exciting romance, *Family Ties*.

Happy Reading!

Anne Canadeo, Senior Editor

Please address questions and book requests to:
Silhouette Reader Service
U.S.: 3010 Walden Ave., P.O. Box 1325, Buffalo, NY 14269
Canadian: P.O. Box 609, Fort Erie, Ont. L2A 5X3

# STAND-IN HUSBAND

## Anne Peters

•

Silhouette
ROMANCE™
Published by Silhouette Books
America's Publisher of Contemporary Romance

To the courageous immigrants
who made this country great

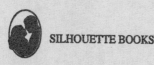 SILHOUETTE BOOKS

ISBN 0-373-19110-3

STAND-IN HUSBAND

**Books by Anne Peters**

Silhouette Romance

*Through Thick and Thin* #739
*Next Stop: Marriage* #803
*And Daddy Makes Three* #821
*Storky Jones Is Back in Town* #850
*Nobody's Perfect* #875
*The Real Malloy* #899
*The Pursuit of Happiness* #927
*Accidental Dad* #946
*His Only Deception* #995
*McCullough's Bride* #1031
*\*Green Card Wife* #1104
*\*Stand-in Husband* #1110

\*First Comes Marriage

Silhouette Desire

*Like Wildfire* #497

## ANNE PETERS

makes her home in the Pacific Northwest with her husband and their dog, Adrienne. Family and friends, reading, writing and travel—those are the things she loves most. Not always in that order, not always with equal fervor, but always without exception.

# MARRIAGE CONTRACT

I, __Joy Marie Cooper__, being of a proud spirit and a need not to feel embarrassed when my EX-fiancé gets married, do hereby propose a temporary marriage with the impossibly sexy, temporarily amnesiac, nearly drowned sailor, __Paul Mallik.__

In return for his acting like a loving husband—in public ONLY—I will help Paul become a United States citizen.

At no time should the issue of love enter into this agreement...unless, of course, he happens to fall in love with me!

Bride's signature *Joy Marie Cooper*

Groom's signature *Paul Mallik*

# Chapter One

All through the night the raging spring storm had battered and shaken the house, rattling shutters and windowpanes till Joy was sure they would give. The racket had kept her awake in spite of the sleeping pill to which she had uncharacteristically resorted in her need for oblivion and rest.

At first light she gave up. Wearily, feeling as brittle and used up as a rusty scouring pad, she dragged herself into the kitchen. The wind had slackened; it was quieter now, but the storm was far from over. The cabin's ancient timbers still groaned and shook and raindrops still peppered its roof and walls like a barrage of pebbles tossed from an enraged giant's hand.

Joy's head hurt. So did her eyes. Too much bawling, she thought, twisting her lips into a self-deriding sneer. Where's that precious pride of yours when you need it, Joy Marie Cooper?

After starting the coffee, Joy stared out the window. Beyond the cabin's shabby stretch of lawn, she could see the stand of gnarled surf pines bowing and bucking beneath the wind's still-considerable force. The dune grass, too, was being whipped this way and that in a mad, frenzied dance. Ominous banks of clouds still obscured the horizon.

A native of Oregon's North Coast, Joy knew that nature's anger, once unleashed, was slow to abate this time of year. Spring storms were legend. This one might well blow on through the rest of the day.

Vern Harris's wedding day!

*Stop it!*

With a snort of vexation, Joy pivoted away from the window. What was keeping that darned coffee anyway?

Oh, hell! she thought an instant later, eyeing the silent coffee maker and its still-empty carafe. The power's out. Lordy, what next?

Massaging her temples, Joy briefly contemplated firing up the old kitchen stove on the closed-in back porch but, on second thought, couldn't quite rise to the occasion. In fact, she suddenly couldn't wait to get out of the house. Yanking off her robe as she went, she strode into the bedroom. She tossed the robe on the bed, snatched up some sweats and dragged them on over her nightshirt.

On the back porch, she shoved her feet into rubber boots and sent the wood stove a baleful glare. She did not look forward to the chore of firing up the relic, but knew she would have no choice if she wanted to eat. There was little chance the power would be back on again before this storm had blown itself out.

Outside, she took a deep breath and eagerly turned her face into the wind. She welcomed the feel of the rain's cool sting on her feverish skin as she marched up the path. Cresting the last dune, she stopped a moment to stare, awestruck, at the wild and foaming sea. Its churning turbulence aptly suited her emotional state, mirrored it in fact. Spreading her arms, she raced down the dune toward it. Running at the edge of the foamy, thundering surf, buffeted by the wind and driven by a new, restless energy, she emptied her mind of every negative thought.

At first, nearly blinded by the rain, she didn't consciously take note of the dark shape up ahead on the strand. When it finally did register, she slowed, shielding her eyes for a better look. What on earth . . . ?

Joy's heart began to race even before her feet once again picked up speed. She ran now in earnest, urged forward by some nebulous sense of dread. Unmindful of the waves that immediately swamped her boots and dragged at her every step, she sloshed out into the surf. She knew that the shape was a person long before her eyes confirmed it.

She also knew that the person was dead.

But knowing this didn't slow her. On the contrary, the realization urged her on. She was close now. There, an arm.

Waist-deep in roiling water and unsteady on her feet, Joy made a desperate lunge for the limb. Her fingers closed around a cold, lifeless hand only to instantly feel it slide out of her grip.

Joy cursed through sobs of frustration. Another wave thundered to shore. It knocked her down like a pin, swamped and tumbled her, and tossed her up onto the sandy beach with bone-jarring force.

Joy clutched at the sand as the receding water sucked at her. Shaking her head to clear it, she scrambled to her knees and could have wept with relief when she spotted the body just a few feet away. It, too, had been swept up and tossed ashore by the incoming breaker.

She scrambled over to it as fast as her waterlogged condition allowed. She was determined to win this fight with the sea, to save this person from a watery grave and give him or her the decent burial she would have wished her father to have.

Another foaming wall of water approached. Without stopping to think or to look, Joy made a blind grab for the nearest limb and staggered out of the surf with the body in tow.

Once completely clear of the water, she dropped what turned out to be one of the feet and collapsed on her knees. On all fours, with her head dangling limply between her hunched shoulders, she spat out saltwater and, for just a moment, concentrated on simply catching her breath. When at last she was able, she rocked back on her heels and raised her head. Slowly, reluctantly now, she prepared to take her first good look at what—whom— she'd found. Man, woman? Old, young? She hardly dared open her eyes and find out.

*Please, not a child,* she silently prayed, then was reminded of how heavy the body had been as she'd dragged it ashore.

*Body.* Joy shuddered at the word's cold and impersonal ring. It wasn't just a body, but a *person* she'd found. Oh, God. The enormity, the horror of it, suddenly hit her like a blow. This was someone's mother, sister, father, son...

She could have wept, would have, when another thought struck: *Are you sure this person is dead?*

Joy's eyes popped open. Jiminy Cricket! Five years as a lifeguard and she hadn't even thought to check!

The first thing she saw, the nearest thing to her, was feet. Big ones. Relief flooded her. This was not a kid. Thank God for that much at least.

She scanned the rest of the body and her eyes widened. This was a man. A man in a wet suit. The garment, clinging like a second skin to a well-muscled torso and other pertinent features, left no room at all for doubt.

So, could he be alive?

Joy scooted up near his head and immediately turned it sideways toward her. She stuck a finger into his mouth and checked for the tongue, making sure it was clear of his throat. Then she gripped his wrist to feel for a pulse even as she leaned forward and put her ear to his mouth. She strained to hear, to *feel*. Was that . . . ?

"Damn!" She couldn't be sure she'd felt anything. If there was a pulse, if there was breathing, it was awfully feeble. And yet . . .

Abruptly, Joy rolled him over, straddled his back, grabbed his elbows and sharply pulled back on his arms. Hold, release, press. Grab, pull, hold, release . . .

"Damn!" she gasped after several more unsuccessful attempts. This maneuver wasn't working, but that didn't mean she was ready to give up. Once the notion that there might be a chance to save this man had taken hold, her well-developed stubborn streak stopped her from relinquishing hope this soon.

Her motions brisk and sure, she flipped the man onto his back again. Pinching his nose, she cupped his mouth with her hand and covered his cold, bloodless lips with her own.

Come on, she thought fiercely as she filled his lungs with her own breath again and again. *Breathe, damn you.* It seemed like forever before her efforts paid off. But it could only have taken a few short, crucial moments until there was a shaky inhalation.

It was followed immediately by a mighty expulsion of air that jerked the man upright. He stared, wild-eyed, coughing and spluttering, and then, once again, he passed out.


So now what? Joy thought, standing beneath the stinging spray of a hot shower and feeling as battered and shell-shocked as her unexpected houseguest undoubtedly did. She'd been trying—in vain so far—to assimilate the incredible thing that had happened. That she, a twenty-six-year-old small-town schoolteacher, had somehow performed a miracle there on that beach totally blew her mind. *She* had given the breath of life to another human being!

Suddenly, the ramifications of that scared the hell out of her!

Because that human being she had saved was a man. A man she had somehow managed to maneuver onto her hastily retrieved surfboard and, travois-fashion, dragged to the house. Whom she had manhandled out of an insulated wet suit and wrestled into bed.

A man who was built like an athlete, who was cold to the bone—not to mention severely shocked—and who, at this very moment, was dead to the world in *her* spare room.

And as if all of that weren't enough, he was a man who was now *her* responsibility!

He was hers to take care of. For the short term at least. And wasn't that just swell!

Joy turned off the shower before the depleted hot water tank could undo the work its heated contents had done and douse her with cold. Hysterical laughter briefly threatened as, shivering in the unheated bathroom, she hastened to dry herself and get dressed. The electricity was still off. The storm still shook the timbers. The entire situation really would be hilarious if it weren't so darned typical of the way her life had been going of late!

Here the last thing she needed was more man problems. Hadn't she escaped her apartment, first to Seattle and then to the cottage, to get away from those in the first place? So what happened? More man problems, of course!

Well, she wasn't going to stand still for it. She would formulate a plan of action.

For starters, she would call the authorities. Joy tugged a heavy sweater over her head. She would let *them* worry about the guy. That was their job. After all, this man, insulated wet suit and all, had to have come from somewhere. It stood to reason he'd be missed. Missed by parents, siblings, friends, a boss. This man was no kid. And he was attractive, in a drowned rat kind of way. There was bound to be a wife or a girlfriend going out of her head with worry.

Right.

Joy slipped into jeans, wool socks and fuzzy slippers. She would call Sheriff Smits and that would be that. They would come fetch him. Probably send an ambulance and, if necessary, stick him in the hospital for a couple of days of observation or something. After which—bingo! Good as new and goodbye, Charlie.

Joy scooped her still-damp hair off her face and into a haphazard ponytail. Having decided on a plan, she felt infinitely better. Until she picked up her bedside phone to call the sheriff and didn't get a dial tone.

A dead phone. Uh-huh.

Joy had to close her eyes and count to ten before she felt composed enough to leave her room. Deciding to check on her ''guest'' on her way to the kitchen phone—maybe the phones weren't really dead; maybe the bedroom extension was just faulty somehow—she detoured to the spare room and carefully inched open the door. She stuck in her head. And immediately jerked back.

The man was awake.

Her first reaction was to close the door again and run. She had the oddest feeling that once she stepped over the threshold, her life would irrevocably change. Which was just ridiculous enough to make her mad. ''Get a grip, girl.''

Right.

On a deep breath, Joy pasted a smile on her face and stuck her head back into the room. ''Hi,'' she said. ''You okay?''

Which, she immediately told herself, had to be one of her stupider questions, given the circumstances. No wonder he didn't deign to answer, but only stared at her.

His eyes were blue, Joy discovered. And amazingly lucid, given what he'd been through.

''I'm Joy Cooper,'' she said, making no move to step into the room. His unblinking gaze trapped her own and, as they studied each other across a lengthening silence, Joy's heart tripped over itself and afterward refused to beat normally again for quite some time.

Though reason told her there was nothing to be afraid of, her feet seemed nailed to the hall floor. It didn't matter that she told herself it made no sense. That the man was helpless. That he was at *her* mercy, not the other way around. And that this weird feeling she had was ridiculous. He wasn't the first man she'd ever had in her house, for crying out loud!

So he was a stranger, so what? She'd never been particularly shy. And she certainly hadn't hesitated earlier, when she'd stripped him naked and—

That was it!

A hot flush suffused her. She had stripped him and, now that he was awake, he was bound to realize it. What was he thinking? His eyes showed nothing. Did he think she'd stopped to ogle his body? Did he resent the invasion of his privacy? Did he...?

The man closed his eyes as if on a spasm of pain, abruptly bringing Joy's fanciful contemplations to a halt.

"What is it?" she asked in alarm, rushing up to the bed. When he didn't answer, she bent over him, gingerly picking up one of his lifeless hands and nervously chafing it between both of hers. Her brow puckered with concern, she peered into his ashen face. "Are you in pain, mister? Can I do something?"

The shake of his head was barely perceptible. Joy might have missed it if she hadn't been watching for his every reaction, however slight. He opened his eyes again and met Joy's anxious gaze. He moved his lips, but no words came out. Joy watched the tip of his tongue slide across lips that were dry and cracked. Earlier, unable to make him drink, she had wiped them with a wet cloth and tried to squeeze some moisture into his mouth that way.

"Are you thirsty?" she asked.

"Y-yes," he croaked haltingly. It was as if he were testing his ability to speak. His eyes were intent on her face. His voice was husky, rough, as if from laryngitis. Too much saltwater.

And, maybe, Joy thought with a rush of compassion, from too many unanswered calls for help. She had a fleeting vision of this man barely afloat and fighting to stay alive in that vast, treacherous and deathly cold

ocean. Calling for help, with no one to hear him above
the roar of wind and waves.

Oh, Pop...

Running to fill a glass with water, Joy drew in a quivering breath. Her father had been lost at sea more than
ten years now, but the thought of how cruelly and alone
he had met his end never failed to make her ache.

She was glad again, suddenly, and proud, that this man
had been spared such a fate with *her* help. And she vowed
to do whatever she possibly could to help bring about his
complete recovery.

Her brief lapse into self-conscious reticence forgotten, she matter-of-factly put her arm beneath the man's
head and gently helped him to drink.

"Easy," she murmured, withdrawing the glass a little
when he would have greedily gulped. "You'll get all you
need, but we don't want you to choke, now do we?"

He didn't speak. But as he drank, his gaze clung to hers
with a hint of something akin to desperation. His obvious vulnerability and need clutched at Joy's tender heart
and, settling him back onto the pillow, she offered him a
genuine smile along with a comforting touch of the hand
to his brow. His skin felt hot, almost feverish.

"You'll be fine." Though worried, Joy spoke softly,
reassuringly, as she might to one of her young pupils.
"I'm sure you will, with a bit of rest."

She would have withdrawn her hand, but he caught it
with his and held it. His lips moved as he strained to
speak. "Th-thank..."

"Ssh." Joy silenced him with her finger. "Just rest.
Don't strain yourself. Are you hungry?"

Again that almost imperceptible shake of the head.

"Well, I'll fix you some soup anyway." This time he didn't stop her from removing her hand as she straightened. His eyelids fluttered and closed on a sigh.

Joy tucked the covers more firmly into the mattress. "You go ahead and sleep while I get the old stove going, all right?"

Sure that he had drifted off, Joy quietly backed away from the bed, all the while chattering in a soothing tone of voice. "Chicken soup would be best, I think. Even out of the can, it's supposed to have restorative qualities. In any case, it couldn't hurt. My mother always says..."

She was near the door. A floorboard creaked.

He opened his eyes and said, "Wait" quite clearly.

Joy froze at the hint of command. Some of her earlier nervousness returned. "Yes?"

"I'm not dead."

Though it was a statement rather than a question, his frown spoke of bewilderment. Somehow this was reassuring to Joy, and she relaxed. "No," she said, "you're not dead."

Sensing that there was more he wanted to say, she moved closer again to stand by the foot of the bed.

"I thought I had died," he said slowly. "Out there..."

"Well, you didn't." Her fingers closed around the bedpost and she shrugged with a self-conscious little grin. "I guess I saved your life. I, uh, found you in the surf and, well, here you are. Alive."

"Alive..."

Their gazes held until, frowning, he carefully moved his head and scanned the room. "Where exactly is *here?*"

Joy found herself fascinated by the way he spoke. So slow. And deliberate. She sensed it had nothing to do with the trauma he'd endured, yet it wasn't exactly a foreign accent she detected, either. More like a formality of speech, a hint of British...

"This is Oregon," she said, and, after a slight pause during which she thought she saw his confusion increase, helpfully added, "You know, the United States of America?"

"Ah."

Joy thought she saw something flicker then in the gaze he returned to her, some indefinable emotion. She asked, "Can you, uh, tell me what happened?"

At her question, his frown increased and his gaze clouded. Puzzled, Joy watched his Adam's apple bob as he swallowed, closed his eyes and, after a moment, mutely shook his head.

Something unpleasant and jittery uncoiled in Joy's stomach, warning her that the situation was about to become more complicated. She told herself she was being silly, that the man's reticence was natural. He was mere hours away from surviving a horrendous ordeal. Was it any wonder he couldn't yet talk about it?

"I'm sorry. Forget it." She let go of the bedpost and moved toward the door. "Rest now and we'll talk later."

"No." He opened his eyes. Meeting hers, they were full of anguish and confusion. In spite of her misgivings, Joy felt a tug on the strings of her ever-bleeding heart. Poor guy, she thought, he's been through hell.

For a moment, as they gazed at each other, neither spoke. Wind-driven rain drummed against the window and the house creaked. And then his lips moved. Joy had to strain to hear him whisper. "I..."

He moistened his lips, visibly struggling with himself before haltingly speaking again. "I think... my name is... P... Pa..." His effort faded into nothingness.

Joy's heart sank. He *thinks* his name is Pa—? What was that? Paul?

"Paul." She said it aloud. "Is that your name? Paul?"

He didn't answer, but Joy took the feeble motion of his head to mean yes.

Oh, boy. Her sense of impending doom mushroomed. This man was in much worse shape than she had feared. Alarm bells clanged in her head as she realized things were definitely about to go from bad to worse. Her mother had always warned her about this habit of dragging home strays. One of these times it'd get her in trouble, she'd always maintained.

"I don't suppose a last name comes to mind?"

Even as she asked the question, Joy knew what the answer was going to be. And so she wasn't even surprised when Paul's only response was another barely perceptible shake of the head.

"Of course not," Joy said to the nearest wall. "That would be too easy, wouldn't it?"

Still, she looked back at Paul and gave it one more try. "Anything?" she asked. "Can you remember anything else at all?"

Reading the answer in the bleak expression on his face, Joy sank down on the edge of the mattress and closed her eyes. "Amnesia," she muttered glumly. "You're right, Ma—one of these times . . . !"

## Chapter Two

The effort of talking had sapped what little strength Paul had had left to spare. A sense of ennui filled him and it became increasingly difficult to remain focused.

"Uh, Paul?"

The woman—had she said her name was Jane?—was addressing him. It took an effort to open his eyes and even more to summon up speech. "Yes?"

"I, uh..."

Poor lady. She sat at the edge of his mattress and was all but wringing her hands. Paul wished he could offer her some kind of reassurance, even promise he would be up and out of her hair in just another moment or two.

But the fact was he was as weak and helpless as a newborn babe. And just as babies were strangers in a strange new world, so it was with him. He was nobody. He knew nothing. Remembered nothing. He had no identity. He had nowhere to go, and there was no one to whom he could turn for help and guidance.

Except her. Jane.

But she was saying, "I think I'd better call the sheriff," in a tone that very much suggested she wanted someone to take him off her hands. Her face was a study of conflicting emotions. Concern warred with unease, uncertainty with determination.

It was the latter that gave him hope. Confused as he was, unable to think clearly or remember anything at all, he nevertheless felt he'd be all right as long as he could rest a bit here with Jane. He was so tired. Everything ached. He longed for sleep, but she was leaving the room, closing the door. Calling the sheriff...

Paul wanted to leap out of bed and stop her, and cursed his battered body for not responding to his will. The word *sheriff* frightened him. It conjured up an armed man on horseback with a tin star pinned to his chest. But what did that mean?

"Ja—" He tried to call out her name. The need to stop her, to explain, question, and to... to beg, if necessary, gave him the strength to raise up on an elbow. He clawed at the blankets and dragged his legs off the bed. The effort drained him. His shout died uncompleted in his throat and he toppled forward as though pushed from behind. He hit the floor headfirst, but never felt the impact.

Joy heard the crash and came running. "What—?" Seeing Paul on the floor, she exclaimed, "Oh, for crying out loud," and rushed over to him.

"What're you trying to do, you foolish man, kill yourself after all the trouble I went to to save your life? What is it with you, a death wish?"

With hands that shook, she gently rolled him onto his back, muttering, "Well, not in my house, buster. I want you out of here, but not dead. Do you hear me?"

It was obvious he didn't. He was unconscious. She frowned at the bloody gash that split his forehead, reached behind herself for a pillow and carefully pushed it beneath his head. She knew there was no way she'd ever be able to get his deadweight up off the floor and back into bed.

Not at all sure for a moment what to do next, she anxiously hovered, staring at him. Who was he, this man she'd fished from the sea? His hair was dark, and cropped short. It was stiff from dried saltwater and sticking out every which way. His bleeding forehead was high and well shaped, as was his nose and the rest of his face.

Why was it that men always seemed to be blessed with luxurious lashes, Joy wondered inconsequentially. Her own, though thick, were so stubby and blond that without mascara they were almost invisible.

Dismissing that, her eyes drifted lower, lingering for a moment on the man's powerful shoulders and partially covered chest. A swimmer's torso, she thought, with the leanness of hip and thighs she knew well were a part of that package. Not because she'd seen Paul naked—she had, of course, but she'd been much too intent on just getting him warm to take notice of any particulars.

No, it was the image of another man's body that came to mind. Another swimmer's body, one she had come to know well in the course of a two-year engagement.

Paul stirred, groaned, and Joy was abruptly recalled from the past to the present. A present that required her to deal with a situation that was rapidly growing beyond her.

"Paul," she called, gently shaking the stranger's shoulder with one hand while placing the other against his cheek in a gesture of comfort that was characteristic of her nurturing nature. Just as she would soothe any of her young charges at school if they had come to harm.

But their skin did not feel as this man's did. Rough from exposure and from the stubble that shadowed his cheeks. And hot. So hot, way hotter than before, it seemed to her.

At her touch, he groaned again. His eyelids, tinged blue with fatigue, fluttered and he restlessly rolled his head from side to side.

"Paul, can you hear me?"

He didn't want to. The blackness from which the woman's voice tried to coax him was warm and...safe. There was danger in leaving it, though he couldn't get a grip on quite what that danger was.

"Paul, please..."

Perhaps it was the note of desperation in the woman's soft voice that got to him. He knew all about desperation.

"I've got to get you off this floor and back into bed."

Warm, sweet breath fanned his face and he felt an arm slide beneath his shoulders. An elusive scent—flowers, woman—enveloped him and he felt her lean into him as her other arm spanned his torso and she tried to raise him up.

"Wait..." He couldn't be sure the word would be heard by her since he couldn't be sure he still had a voice.

The press of her breasts against his chest eased a bit but she didn't release him. "Yes...?"

He opened his eyes to find hers—anxious and wide—a scant inch or two from his own. He moved his head and their noses touched. He was beyond reacting to the intimacy of it and, apparently, the woman was, too. Her anxious gaze never wavered from his.

"Leave me...here," he managed to croak. "For now. I...I...can't..." He had no reserves left to draw from; there was no way he could help her move or lift him.

She seemed to realize it, too. She withdrew her arms and straightened, leaving him with a sense of abandonment so acute, he gripped her hand to make her stay. Somehow, touching her seemed to anchor him in reality, and that nameless, nebulous fear he felt seemed less with her close. He tried to tell her so, but all he could utter was an inarticulate sound that she answered with a wobbly smile of reassurance.

She patted his hand and extricated herself from his grip. "I'm only going to cover you with this comforter..." She tugged one off the bed and tucked it around him and beneath his chin. "...and then I'll tend to that gash."

"Please..." His fingers caught at her sweater. "Don't...need...doctor...no...sheriff..."

She searched his eyes and must have been reassured or, at least, moved by his entreaty. She relaxed and let her expression turn wry.

"Don't worry," she said. "As it turns out, I couldn't call anybody if I wanted to. The storm knocked the power out—as per usual—and the phone's dead, too."

She sounded philosophical rather than upset. Relief at the respite drained the last of Paul's reserves. He would sleep now, he thought, his mind already blurring. And he'd...plan...later....

On a long, unsteady sigh, he subsided back into oblivion.

Joy contemplated her guest's supine form for another moment. It looked like she was stuck with him, and with whatever responsibility caring for him entailed. Until her utilities were restored, at least. Not one to rail against matters that were beyond her control, Joy issued a resigned sigh and got up to go fetch her first-aid kit.

On her way out the door, a dark heap on the floor on the other side of the bed caught her eye. Paul's survival suit and undershorts.

She detoured and gingerly picked up each item. Though not dripping, they were still wet and had left a damp stain on the braided rug.

Thinking she'd best hang the insulated suit up to dry for the time being, Joy carried the bundle out to the back porch. She would throw the things in the washing machine once the power was back on.

In the act of hanging them up, a thought occurred to her. Might there be a label or a name tag or something that could offer a clue to Paul's identity?

She shook the neoprene suit out and held it at arm's length. With narrowed eyes she studied it. And sure enough, there. On the left front. MALLIK. The word—name?—had been stitched right into the material the way ballplayers' names or club logos were stitched into hats and uniforms. Except these letters were plainer, not fancy or cursive, just no-nonsense capitals.

MALLIK.

Brow creased, Joy contemplated the word. It meant nothing to her. So she decided it had to be his name. Bingo!

Her expression cleared on a grin that expanded into a triumphant little laugh. Because not only was she willing to bet now that Mallik was indeed the man's name, no— the fact that it was stitched into the garment very likely meant he was part of some seafaring team or organization.

Which meant that the next logical step was for her—
no, no, she corrected herself—for the *police* to draw up
a list of nonfishing, seagoing organizations.

She had already eliminated the possibility that Paul
was a fisherman; his hands were too soft and well kept.
No calluses. But there were all kinds of ships on the
ocean. Which meant that all the police would have to do
was figure out which of those ships had been in this area
during the storm. After which, presto—goodbye, unin-
vited houseguest.

On the other hand—practicality forced Joy to consider all angles—failing the above, the mere act of going
over such a list with Paul might very well prod his memory. Especially since they now knew his family name, too.

Encouraged, Joy meticulously went over the rest of the
garment but aside from a rather generic manufacturer's
label, the words *Made In Korea,* and an XL that told her
what she already knew—namely that Paul was a big
man—there was nothing.

Oh, well. With a mental shrug, Joy hung the garment
up on a nail. She consoled herself that, after all, it wasn't
like she had expected to find the man's wallet or anything. There weren't any pockets in the wet suit. Good
enough that she had found *something*.

She hugged herself against a sudden, violent shiver,
which brought home to her just how cold it had grown
out here in the porch. In the whole house, for that matter. If she didn't do something about heat pretty quick,
her guest might succumb to hypothermia yet.

She hurried into a slicker and, head ducked against the
still-raging elements, made several runs to the woodshed
and back. By the time she had hauled in as much wood
as she figured she would need to keep the stove and the
living room fireplace going for the day, water was sluic-

ing off the slicker into her boots and she was almost as
wet again as she'd been after the rescue.

After stopping only long enough to shed slicker, boots
and sodden socks, Joy labored over firing up the stove.
It had been a while, both for her and the stove, but at last
the kindling took flame.

She opened a can of chicken soup and put it on to heat,
likewise a large kettle of water and her grandmother's
dented old percolator.

On her way to her room to change, she looked in on
Paul. He lay exactly as she'd left him, but he was breathing deeply in sleep. Best thing for him, Joy decided, but
reminded herself that his forehead still needed attention.

She raced into her room, shivered her way out of her
wet things and into some dry, and hurried back out to the
porch. The tantalizing aroma of chicken soup made her
mouth water and her stomach rumble, bringing home to
her the fact that she hadn't eaten yet that day. What time
had it gotten to be anyway?

Who knew? There was no clock on the porch, her
watch was in the bedroom and the kitchen clock was
electric. Dismissing the subject as irrelevant, Joy moved
soup and coffee away from direct heat to a warming spot
and went into the living room to fire up the hearth.

That done, she checked on Paul once again. He still
hadn't stirred. Joy studied him, worrying her lip as she
wondered if he was warm enough down on the floor. He
had no clothes on and only a braided cotton rug separated his naked flesh from the cold, drafty floor. The
comforter was fine for on top.... Should she wake him?
Try to get him back into bed?

Her reluctance to once again touch a stranger's nude
flesh fueled her indecision. Should she try to move him
into the living room? Feed him? What?

How exhausted he still looked. Joy told herself that was the reason she was leaving him where he was for a little while longer. The gash on his forehead, too, would keep. It had crusted over. He'd be okay.

Thus assuaging her conscience, Joy crept from the room, leaving the door ajar so she could hear him if he called.

Starving, suddenly, she went and got herself some soup and a cup of coffee. She took them into the living room where it was warm.

She settled herself in the old recliner next to the hearth, snuggled an afghan around herself and, for the first time in what seemed like an eternity, allowed herself to relax. The spare room was right next to the living room, and both doors were open. Should he need her, she could be with Paul in seconds.

Staring into the flames, Joy succumbed to a sudden, overwhelming fatigue as the sleepless night, as well as the events of the morning, caught up with her. Slowly she relaxed in the capacious chair and sipped her soup. Warmth spread through her. Life tingled back into cold-numbed fingers and toes in contrast to her mind, which went vacant.

A sigh trembled up from somewhere deep within, and her eyelids drooped. She set the soup bowl aside, and then she slept.

Acrid smoke. Paul stirred restlessly, tossing his head from side to side in an effort to elude the fumes that were clogging his nostrils and throat. "No," he mumbled. "No..."

And then he shouted, "Annaaa...!" and surged up-right. Choking and coughing, he wildly looked around.

Where was he? He had been dreaming. Anna. Miguel.
That fire . . . !

A fit of coughing seized him. *"Donda mutto!"* This
was no dream. This smoke was real. The woman!

Suddenly frantic, Paul tossed off the comforter. Pan-
ic-induced adrenaline was a powerful fuel. He was on his
feet and running in one swift move. Through the door.
Smoke blinded him, choked him, but guided him, too. It
was thicker over there, through that doorway.

Paul clamped a hand over his nose and plunged in.
Over there, a fireplace. And smoke, black and lethal,
billowing out in clouds while a roar like a freight train
came from inside the chimney.

*Santo Dio.* Swaying on his feet, it didn't occur to him
to wonder why he'd thought the imprecation in some
foreign tongue. There was a chimney fire!

The realization had barely taken hold when a cascade
of water erupted from the hearth with an explosive hiss
and sizzle that was immediately followed by another
noxious emission of smoke.

Without conscious direction, Paul charged out of the
room and out onto the enclosed back porch where he
collided smartly with the lady of the house. Their colli-
sion sent a geyser of water spraying out of the bucket she
carried, icily dousing Paul's bare legs and feet.

"What's happening?" Paul gasped, doing an awk-
ward little dance away from the water while, at the same
time, trying to hold Joy still and check her out. "Are you
all right?"

"I'm fine." Joy brushed off his hands, taking no time
to stop in her mad dash back into the living room. She
had just scrambled down off the roof to fill another
bucket with water; this one she planned to dump into the

fireplace. "But what in tarnation are you doing up and out here?"

"Fire . . . ! Must rescue you."

"Rescue me?" Joy tossed back over her shoulder. She figured one more dousing oughta do it, and heaved-ho. "You can barely stand up."

She was right. Back on the porch, Paul blinked his burning eyes. He raked a shaky hand through his hair, momentarily at a loss.

Though it seemed to him he should be taking some sort of meaningful action, he couldn't seem to move or get a clear grip on what he ought to do. The adrenaline rush was receding as rapidly as it had flared, leaving him dizzy and spent.

Paul laid a palm against the nearest wall for support. Spying a chair, he tottered toward it and plopped himself down. In the aftermath of panic, he felt awful. His head pounded. Resting elbows on knees, he leaned forward and buried his perspiration-slick face in his hands.

The rattle of the empty bucket made him raise his head a fraction. The woman, blurred by his fuzzy vision, stood in the doorway. She was weaving back and forth. Or maybe he was the unsteady one?

Their eyes met. Hers were wide with shock in a soot-blackened face.

"I can't believe this is happening," Joy rasped, her throat sore from inhaled smoke. She took the two steps down from the kitchen and sank onto the lower step. The bucket dropped out of her limp grip and hit the floor with a clatter that went unheeded.

With the air between them a smoky curtain that half shrouded their forms, Joy and Paul stared at each other in shell-shocked silence. Though the wind howled and raindrops danced a rapid tap on the roof and windows of the porch, neither was aware of it.

"Who *are* you?" Joy finally whispered hoarsely, hugging her knees when a shiver shook her frame in spite of the warmth radiating from the old-fashioned cookstove. "*What* are you? Some kind of a jinx?"

# Chapter Three

Paul heard the woman speak, but was beyond comprehending the words. Hunched into himself, it was taking all of his rapidly waning strength and concentration just to remain upright on that chair.

The woman's eyes, so wide and unblinkingly focused on his, were like a lifeline to sanity. As his senses whirled, he clung to them with ever-increasing desperation. His thoughts were a maelstrom of uncertainty and fear. His emotions took turns being raw one moment and then numb. Reality blended with memories and dreams until he no longer knew which was which. Or who this woman was whose eyes seemed to demand so much from him though he was able to give so little. To give nothing, in fact. Because he was nothing. He was nobody. *Nobody...*

*Santo Cristo!*

Paul buried his face in his hands as a sob, deep and

wrenching, broke from the depth of his bewildered despair.

At the sound of it, Joy leapt to her feet. She was deeply distressed yet knew instinctively that what was happening was an inevitable, and perhaps necessary, delayed reaction to the trauma Paul had endured.

Grabbing the nearest thing at hand—a seaman's pea jacket that had once been her father's—she tucked it around him. And then she gathered him into her arms and held him, soothed him, until she felt the tremors that racked him subside.

"I . . ." Paul felt weak as a kitten. Though he'd managed to pull himself together, he sensed that his grip on his emotions was tenuous at best. The woman's arms around him were a comfort, but he knew it was weak of him to want to keep them there. He was a man.

"Forgive me."

"Don't." Joy hushed him. "Please don't say anymore. There's nothing to forgive, believe me. You're just all done in, and no wonder. Come on—"

She rose from her crouched position and urged him up, as well. "Let's find you something to wear and get out of here."

Too dazed to resist, Paul allowed himself to be helped to his feet. He felt far removed from himself and curiously boneless. He clutched the jacket the woman had draped around his shoulders, his entire body now one big shiver that caused his teeth to chatter like castanets.

Aware of Paul's precarious state, Joy wasted no time getting him out of the porch. She put her arm around his waist and placed one of his arms across her shoulders. None too steady herself after the scare of the fire and everything that followed, she nevertheless managed to maneuver him back into the smoke-filled house.

Passing through the kitchen, she snatched a couple of tea towels off the towel rack. "Here." She pressed one into Paul's free hand. "It's going to get pretty noxious, so hold that to your mouth and nose."

Circumventing the living room, as well as the spare room, they made their slow way into Joy's bedroom. Once there, Joy made Paul sit on the edge of her bed, flipping its quilt up around his shivering form for additional warmth while she rummaged in her closet. Shortly she emerged with a man's lined jogging suit, slightly shabby, but clean. She also dug some men's shorts and T-shirt out of a drawer and handed them to Paul without explaining whose they were. Paul was too wrung-out to either ask or care.

On her part, Joy didn't spare a thought for propriety, either. She figured they were both operating on automatic pilot and, for now at least, were beyond the conventions customarily observed between strangers. Without fuss, she turned her back, stripped off her clothes and, for the third time that day, stepped into clean jeans, socks and sweater.

Turning around again, she saw that Paul had gotten nowhere in the getting-dressed department. Clearly, he was at the very edge of collapse once again.

"Here, let me." Joy took the clothes out of his hand. She met with no resistance. "Just hang in there a little bit longer if you can," she urged, her throat raw and aching from the smoke she had inhaled and swallowed. Her chest, too, hurt like the dickens.

How much more this poor man must hurt, she thought sympathetically as she gently slipped the T-shirt over his head and, like a mother to her child, stuffed his arms into the short sleeves. Strange, she mused abstractedly, the things we're capable of when the chips are down. And how complaisant we become when we're as needy as this man is right now. Because she had no doubt about one thing. Under ordinary circumstances this was not a man who would willingly relinquish autonomy. Evidence of that was etched in every line of his proud face.

"Just as soon as we get you dressed," Joy said, bending to guide each of his legs into the underpants, "we're out of here. Hold on to me," she instructed moments later, tugging the shorts upward, "and stand up so I can get these past your hips."

Paul complied like a docile robot, neither speaking nor showing an outward reaction of any kind. As efficiently as years of experience volunteering at the hospital as well as teaching primary school had made her, Joy got him into the jogging suit, as well. It was too short in the sleeves and legs, but otherwise fit him adequately well. Paul was pale, his skin clammy with sweat yet cold to the touch, by the time they were done.

Joy, too, was exhausted and drenched in perspiration from the effort.

"Here," she said, her breath labored. "You rest." She pushed him back onto the bed, wishing that someone might be there to minister to *her* needs, as well. She resolutely shook off the momentary weakness and again covered him with the quilt.

"I'll go make sure all the fires are out," she said. "And then I'll warm up the car. Be right back."

Paul didn't ask where they would be going. Nor did he know how long she was gone as he drifted in and out of awareness.

In the living room, Joy cast a despairing look around. Thick, acrid smoke still cloaked the air and made it a punishment to breathe. The place was a mess. Wet soot and ashes had sprayed over everything within a six-foot

radius of the hearth, courtesy of the blasts of water she'd
aimed down the chimney from up on the shallow roof. It
had been the only thing she'd thought of to do after she'd
been so rudely awakened by the smoke.

She remembered thinking, Jiminy Cricket! Ma was
right! That chimney did need cleaning!

It had been one of those typically inane things that always seemed to pop into her mind at times of crisis.

Recollection of the brilliant remark she had made to
Vernon, when he'd told her about getting Sheila pregnant and doing the honorable thing, could still make her
cringe.

*I guess that means our wedding's off, then, huh?*

Honestly! Joy rolled her eyes in self-disgust. The way
her mind worked sometimes, it was a wonder that, in the
end, she always seemed to manage *somehow* to acquit
herself.

In this case, without a phone, calling the fire department had been out. But since she'd had no intention of
letting her much-mourned grandmother's cherished
home of a lifetime burn to the ground, she had uttered a
brief prayer of thanks for single-story construction and
vine-covered trellises and had scrambled up the latter
with garden hose in hand.

Thanks to the rain that had long since soaked the ce-
dar shakes, the roof had not caught fire. Otherwise, her
admittedly unorthodox technique would hardly have
done the trick.

Now Joy looked around once again and, with a shud-
der, consigned the mess and its cleanup to some unspe-
cified time in the future. Ever since inheriting the cottage
some eighteen months ago, she'd planned to redecorate
but had never had the time. Perhaps fate had forced her
hand. And with Vern out of the picture—

Forget Vern, she thought impatiently. The guy's history. It was that darned *merman* she had dragged in off the beach who'd be cramping her style if she didn't get him off her hands, and quickly.

As she thought of him, her brow puckered with a mixture or worry and vexation. The poor guy badly needed rest and recuperation, sure. But why the heck should *she* be saddled with the task of seeing he got it? She had her own agenda and it didn't include playing nursemaid to a man who couldn't even remember his name.

She had saved his life—what more could anyone—could he—ask of her?

Nothing, Joy told herself stoutly, and marched onto the porch to make sure the log in the stove, too, had been reduced to glimmering ashes. Gun-shy, she emptied the coffeepot into the grate as insurance and wrinkled her nose at the resultant, malodorous sizzle. Trust her to pollute the only remaining spot in the house that didn't already stink to high heaven!

It was a relief to escape into the rain. Joy greedily sucked in the bracing sea air, standing for a moment with her head tipped back to offer her hot, sooty face to the cleansing wet. It would be sheer pleasure to take a long, hot shower back at her apartment in town.

Suddenly in a hurry to get there, she sprinted to her car, a modest domestic compact, parked beneath the makeshift carport Vern had always promised to convert into a proper garage.

Another unkept promise...

The heck with that. Joy yanked open the car door. The day would come when she would thumb her nose at Vernon Harris, Sheila MacKenzie and all the darned gossip hounds in the town of Seacrest. Then *she* would have the last laugh!

Savoring the thought, Joy slid behind the wheel and started the engine.

To Paul, it was all a blur. Getting dressed, getting out of the cottage, getting into the car. The drive into Astoria. Everything. His mind was fuzzy, his thoughts flitted from this thing to that like hares on the run. He was warm, bundled into the quilt from the woman's... From—

Why the devil could he never remember her name? Jane...

See Jane run. See Jack run. Jack and Jane went up the hill— No, that was wrong. Paul and Jane went up the hill. There were many hills here, it seemed. And how hot is was....

Paul wrestled out of the quilt. He was burning up. Burning up... Burning...

Fire. *Fire!* Oh, *Dio*—

"Annaaa...!"

"Holy cow!" Joy almost drove off the road, Paul's cry from behind her startled her so. She slammed on the brake, pulled onto the shoulder and whipped around to where he restlessly tossed on the back seat.

"Paul! What happened? Are you all right?" She stretched to put her palm to his forehead. It practically sizzled. "Oh, no." The poor man was burning up with fever.

"Paul..." Gently Joy slid her hand down to his stubbled jaw and urged his face around to hers. "Not that I want to get rid of you—"

*Yes, you do,* a nasty little voice whispered in her head. Joy grimly ignored it.

"—or anything, but wouldn't it be better if I dropped you off at the hospital? You're sick—"

That's as far as she got.

Paul gripped her wrist. "No..." His eyes, bright with fever, were full of pain and entreaty. "Please, Jane..."

*Jane?*

The man really *was* delirious. Yet lucid enough to have understood her and to plead his case. Whatever that was. In any event, his obvious desperation moved Joy sufficiently to concede, with a sigh, "All right, Paul. Relax. No hospital."

She tugged her wrist out of his grip and, grimly wondering if she wasn't being a prime patsy, turned frontward again.

"And...Jane," she heard Paul whisper hoarsely as she put the car in gear, "please. No...sheriff...?"

Pulling out into traffic, Joy could *feel* his eyes boring into her. Beseeching her. Grimly she met his gaze in the rearview mirror and reluctantly nodded her assent even as she questioned her own sanity for giving in to his pleas. What if the man was putting her on with this amnesia bit? What if he was a wanted criminal and *that's* why he didn't want her to call in the law?

Joy darted another glance into the mirror at Paul's waxen face and stark expression. And called herself an idiot. The man was clearly in dire straits, both physically and emotionally. Period. What he needed right now truly wasn't the law, but a friend.

And, like it or not, at the moment she was the only candidate for that position on the ballot.

There comes a time when you've got to trust your gut, Ma, she silently told her mother whose warning about the perils of taking in strays once again rang in her ears.

Joy's gut told her this man was good. She shot him another glance and dryly added to herself, "In any case,

girl, even if he isn't, right now he's too pooped to be
bad.''

Getting him out of her car in front of her house in Astoria presented another challenge. Joy didn't know how
many more challenges she and Paul could handle.

"Here," she said, standing on the curb and leaning
into the back seat. "Whyn't you put your arm around my
neck so I can help get you on your feet?"

It took a bit of maneuvering in the course of which
they touched cheeks more than once, but Joy figured by
now they'd grown well beyond shyness. Which was why
she was more than a little disconcerted and ashamed to
find herself reacting to the feel of Paul's body pressed
against the length of hers when she finally had him upright on the sidewalk.

They stood face-to-face, the need to support Paul until he could master his wobbly legs and make them obey
locking them into a loverlike embrace. With Joy's arms
clasping his taut waist and Paul's around her neck and
shoulder, they stood until Paul could stop swaying.

Joy, tense as a bowstring with unwelcome awareness,
angrily told herself to get a grip, to grow up. When her
traitorous body continued to tingle, she prayed fervently
for the feeling to pass—quickly. And unnoticed by him.

She tilted her head back for a nervous peek into Paul's
face and saw her hopes dashed in overbright, glittering
eyes that mirrored what she felt and then some. As their
gazes collided, he lowered his head toward hers.

Good *grief*. Joy's throat went dry as dust. She closed
her eyes and swallowed. And went rigid with shock at the
feather-soft touch of Paul's lips against hers.

A cry of protest rose into her throat. She let go of his
waist to push against him.

But as, with a groan, Paul covered her mouth completely in the most fervent and desperate kiss Joy had ever experienced, the protest became a whimper of need and her traitorous hands clutched rather than pushed.

Paul's tongue slipped into her mouth and entwined with her own. Locked tightly together, their bodies swayed as one. Their heartbeats went wild in a matching tempo.

The kiss lasted forever but, at the same time, was all too brief. Soon, too soon for Joy's rioting senses, the flare of passion gentled to a series of nuzzling pecks. And then, their breathing still labored, they drew apart to solemnly gaze into each other's eyes.

Joy's knees quaked as Paul tenderly rubbed his thumb back and forth across her lower lip. He murmured soft words. They were unintelligible to Joy, but their musical huskiness stirred her nonetheless.

Until he said, "Anna. Oh, Anna . . ." and bent to kiss Joy again.

"Oh, no, you don't!"

The name he uttered with such tenderness doused the flame of Joy's passion as effectively as the water she'd earlier dumped into the hearth. She jerked her now-flaming face aside, inwardly cringing with embarrassment over her inappropriate behavior of moments ago.

There was no excuse for it, though that certainly wasn't the case for Paul. *He* was ill, delirious with fever, out of his head. He couldn't be blamed for mistaking her for someone else. His wife, perhaps, or his . . . lover.

She—Joy—on the other hand, had taken advantage of the situation and given in to a surge of completely inappropriate lust.

But what was worse was that even now, as Paul's kiss landed moist and hot against the side of her averted head, Joy felt herself lusting still.

"Cut it out," she said crossly, briefly struggling with Paul who was still determined and primed for romance.

The horn of a car blared. "Joy Marie! Hey!" someone shouted.

Joy jumped as though hit by a shot of live current. Feeling as guilty as a schoolgirl caught by Mom doing something illicit, she wrenched her head around and encountered the grinning visage of George Harris, Vernon's brother and designated best man at today's nuptials. Next to him sat his plumpish wife, Caroline. George was leaning out of the window of a pom-pom-and-flower-bedecked sedan. The bridal automobile.

"How's it goin', Joy Marie?" he hollered, salacious curiosity in every line of his face.

For an instant, shocked, Joy couldn't speak. All she could do was stare at the festively decorated car and its formally attired occupants and think, It was *my* wedding those decorations were bought for, you traitor.

But then her gaze snapped to George and she thought she saw pity mixed in with his curious stare. Her chin came up.

"Never better, George," she called with all the cheer she could muster. "Yourself?"

"Fair." George nodded toward Paul. "Say, who's your friend?"

"Friend?" Joy glanced at Paul who stood in a daze, then back again at George with what she hoped was a convincingly dazzling smile. "Why, George, haven't you heard?"

"Heard what?"

"That I'm married. This is my husband."

"Husband? Jeez, Joy Marie...." George and Caroline's thunderstruck expressions were everything Joy could have hoped for with her impulsive declaration. "We all thought—"

"That I'd pine after your brother forever?" Joy trilled a laugh of simulated amusement. She shook her head, as if to say, You poor sap. "Wish him well for me, will you, George?"

George, frowning, waved a hand and drove off, taking with him Joy's impromptu bravado. Though the entire encounter couldn't have lasted more than a minute, she felt as if she had aged ten years. With a choked mutter—half curse, half sob—she unlocked her quaking knees and subsided against Paul.

Not too steady on his feet himself, Paul tottered back a few steps, but tightened his arms around Joy and held her close.

"Anna," he murmured, which was the last thing Joy needed to hear.

"I told you to cut it out," she flared, wrenching herself out of his embrace. "And let's get the heck off of this sidewalk and into the house before someone else I know happens by."

None too gently she proceeded to negotiate Paul's now-unresisting body toward the house. She couldn't believe what she had just done—*said*—to George Harris. The news of her marriage would be all over Seacrest by nightfall. Lord.

"Come on, help me," she huffed as she half pushed, half pulled her disoriented charge up the first steep flight of concrete steps. They were followed by another set of twelve wooden ones that ended in front of the rickety rooming house's olive-green front door.

It was opened from the inside while Joy, winded from the effort of dragging Paul up two dozen steps and beginning to sag beneath his weight, still one-handedly fumbled for her key.

"I been watching you from my window," said her landlady, Mrs. Ross. Disapproval pinched her face and laced each word.

Oh, Lordy me. Another crisis. With an inward groan, Joy closed her eyes for a fortifying moment, then opened them wide with an ultrabright smile. "Gee, thanks for getting the door, Mrs. R."

Edna Ross barely nodded, Joy's sarcasm went way over her head. Her bespectacled eyes sized up Paul, and their expression left no doubt she found him lacking.

"Another friend of yours?" she queried archly, taking her time stepping aside so that Joy and her burden could pass.

"Hmm."

"I believe you're aware that I don't hold with intoxication in this house."

"No problem." Joy helped the badly listing Paul across the threshold. "Haven't touched a drop."

"Hmph."

Joy ignored that. She knew full well the crotchety old lady expected some sort of explanation, but she wasn't about to offer her one till she'd had time to review the exchange with George and formulate a concrete plan. Neither of which she was up to right at the moment. She was exhausted, both mentally and physically. If only she could escape to her apartment upstairs without further delays.

But old lady Ross wasn't done with her yet. "This is a respectable house, young lady," she said, prissily pursing her wrinkled mouth. "I'll remind you that I don't hold with all these comings and goings."

"I know, Mrs. R. I know." Joy knew it did no good to argue with Edna. She tightened her grip on Paul and began to edge him toward the stairs. "It's just that this is an emergency. My, uh, um . . ."

Aw, hell. In for a dime, in for a dollar.

". . . my *husband* here has just suffered a . . . um . . ."

A what? Joy's mind was a whirling blank. But then inspiration mercifully struck. Mrs. Ross's beloved only son had been an epileptic.

". . . an epileptic seizure," she finished. "He'll be fine once I get him upstairs."

"Husband?" Edna exclaimed. "Seizure?" Visibly agitated, she loudly drew breath for further interrogation. But Joy was beyond patience and caring.

"Just one more flight of stairs," she murmured to Paul. "Can you make it?"

He barely managed a nod.

"I'm not so sure I can," Joy muttered as, after a quick "Excuse us" to her bristling landlady, she half shoved, half carried Paul up the stairs to the door of her second-floor apartment.

"Young lady . . . !" Edna Ross called indignantly from the floor of the stairs. "There are rules in this house!"

Joy stifled a curse. "Later, Mrs. R.," she called, propping Paul against the wall, holding him there with the flat of one hand pressed against his chest while unlocking the door and pushing it open with the other. After once more gathering him close, they stumbled inside.

Her bedroom door—mercifully ajar—was on their immediate right. They all but fell through it and onto the queen-size bed.

They lay in a tangle of limbs. Joy's chest heaved as she struggled to catch her breath. With her cheek pressed against Paul's chest she could both feel and hear the slam of his erratically beating heart.

She lifted her head and, gently disentangling herself, got to her feet. Her body quivered with protest. One look at Paul told her he had passed out or fallen asleep. Whatever, he was there to stay. No way did she have it in her to move him even one more inch. It took all of her willpower, and the knowledge that Edna Ross might well tromp upstairs after them, to make herself go and shut the apartment door.

Every motion an effort, she tugged her grandfather's boots off Paul's feet, then dragged off his jacket, and her own. Kicking off her own shoes, too, she stretched out on the bed next to Paul. Her last conscious act was to reach back, grab the bedspread and yank it up over both of them.

It seemed like only minutes later that Joy came awake with a start. Momentarily disoriented, she stared at the ceiling, murky with dusk. Or was it dawn? What had awakened her?

Paul?

She realized then that she was cold. That the bedspread had been tossed aside and that Paul was no longer on the bed next to her. Where had he gone?

Alarmed, Joy sat up. "Paul?"

"Right here, Jane."

Joy whipped her head to the left, toward the sound of Paul's voice. Her eyes widened and she gasped in shock. For Paul was standing on the far side of the bed, tall and imposing, and with his hands resting on his narrow hips. Naked.

Naked and fully aroused.

## *Chapter Four*

*Oh my gosh!*

"P-Paul?" Joy spluttered, aghast, but unable to tear her gaze away from Paul's impressive manly physique. "Wh-what . . . ?"

"I never sleep with my clothes on," he said, very calmly, sounding not in the least self-conscious about his nudity. He just stood there . . .

. . . And gazed at her, Joy realized with a jolt when at last she managed to drag her eyes up to his face. To his eyes. Which gave her another shock.

For even in the twilight, they glittered with an unnatural sheen that bespoke high fever. But also desire. Unmistakable desire.

Joy shivered in response to it. Strangely, she wasn't frightened, but crossed her arms across her chest in an instinctively self-protective gesture just the same.

"*Eposa mu.*" Paul's huskily murmured words were in a language that was, to Joy, reminiscent of Spanish, yet

different enough for her not to understand it. His into-
nation was more easily understood; it was at once ques-
tioning and tender. Nor did it change when he said, in his
formal, Anglo-flavored English, "My wife. I want to
make love with you."

Bending, he put one knee and both hands on the bed.

Oh my gosh, Joy thought, frantically casting around
for a tactful way to dissuade him while keeping a wary
eye on his progress across the bed. Oh my gosh....

"Y-you're ill," she squeaked as his other knee hit the
mattress and he leaned toward her with a heart-stopping
smile that, in Joy, threatened outright cardiac arrest.

"You can't do this!" she entreated, and, as he lunged
forward, flung herself off the bed. She whirled to face
him. "Please, Paul."

Only to realize that the threat had passed. Sprawled
full-length on his face in naked splendor, her amorous
*husband* was dead to the world once again.

Quivering with reaction, Joy leaned back against the
wall and pressed a hand to her heart. She released a
tremulous breath. Phew, that was close!

Of its own accord, her gaze skimmed his recumbent
form, lingered, warmed. A shiver flicked across her skin,
raising goose bumps. Nerves, she told herself. Fatigue.
Or maybe just a plain chill. Certainly it had nothing to do
with sexual awareness or anything. Goodness...

She swallowed against the dryness in her throat, recalling his words. "My wife," he had called her. And those
foreign words he had spoken...

She frowned. Who was he? And could it be he actually *believed* they were married?

Could it be that he had been lucid and aware enough
out there on that sidewalk to have comprehended her exchange with George Harris? And could he have forgot-

ten his own past so completely that he'd accepted her statement as gospel?

Joy's knees quaked and she slid down the wall into a crouch. She bit down on the the knuckles of her forefinger and thought, What had she done? And how in the world should she go about undoing it?

Staring at the man on her bed, she gnawed her knuckle to the bone while she contemplated her predicament. Telling George she was married had been an act of impulse. A—in retrospect—probably childish attempt to salvage her pride. As in, Nah, nahnah, nah, nah—see how little Vern's cheap betrayal meant to me?

By now, everyone in town would have heard of her "marriage." By tomorrow at the latest, the news would have spread to Seacrest—and her family.

Panic clutched at Joy's heart. She bit down harder on the abused knuckle. Because it struck her that there was no way she could undo what she had done. No way could she hope to get out of this tangled web with even a shred of pride, dignity and credibility intact.

Oh, boy. Joy dropped her hand and blew out a long and shaky breath. Good old act-first-think-later Joy Marie Cooper had done it again.

Well. Joy pushed herself up on her feet. Under the circumstances there was only one thing she could do—brazen it out. There'd be a fuss—from her brothers, if not from Ma—but she could handle that. As long as she could come up with a plausible story.

And Paul?

Paul. Keeping a thoughtful eye on him, Joy shuffled to the closet, took out a blanket and gently spread it over him.

She decided that Paul, too, she could handle. As long as he didn't remember who he really was, he would believe whatever she told him, right?

Right.

And if he did remember?

Pushing the thought aside, Joy went into the living room and collapsed upon the sofa. One thing at a time, she told herself. Soon enough to worry about glitches when they occurred.

Paul blinked against the brightness. It hurt his eyes and he quickly shut them again. But he was awake. His mind was alert. He knew where he was. Oregon. United States of America. He knew he had not drowned after...

He frowned. After what?

No answer came. Impatiently, he dismissed the question and concentrated instead on the positives.

There was a woman. Flaxen hair, a white smile. She said she had found him in the surf, rescued him. She was warm, safe. This was her house.

Jane.

But... Something else. Smoke. Fire...? Once again, his mind balked.

Cautiously, with a lot of blinking to adjust to the light, Paul once again opened his eyes. A ceiling. White. And a light fixture, a squarish bowl of milky glass. No light shone from there, yet the room was very bright.

Paul rolled his head toward the source of that brightness. A window. He flinched at the stab of pain in his forehead but, touching a finger to the sore spot, nevertheless smiled at the sunshine. Somehow it seemed like a good omen.

Another discomfort made itself felt. He wondered which way lay the bathroom. Scanning the walls, he counted two doors. One stood ajar to what was obviously a corridor. With luck, the other door would lead to where he needed to go.

Cautiously, grimacing at sore bones and stiff joints, Paul levered himself upright. He closed his eyes against an attack of vertigo and waited, breathing deeply, for the spell of light-headedness to pass before inching off the bed. It was a four-poster. Ornately carved dark wood and very wide.

Much wider than the one he and Anna had used to share once upon a time.

The thought came out of nowhere and left him shaken. Anna? Who...?

Paul's head pounded. He clung to a bedpost and stopped a moment to stockpile rapidly waning strength. What a lot of fuzziness there was. Images popped in and out of his mind, but never lingered long enough for him to get a grip on. Something about a ship. And monstrous walls of water.

Was that how he had nearly drowned?

Thoughts. They were a mixture of two languages, both equally familiar, equally natural and clear. He shook his head. Bits and pieces.

He shivered, and realized that he was naked.

*Donde!* Where were his clothes? Ah. His eyes lit on the pile of discarded clothing on the floor. He had taken them off. And why not? He always slept in the nude. Funny he should remember that when so many more important facts eluded him.

At the sink in the bathroom, after his most pressing needs had been assuaged, he stared in shock at the bruised and unsavory image of himself in the mirror. His face was a stubbled and grimy mess. Still, it was an image he recognized. Though his superiors well might not.

Startled blue eyes stared back at him from the mirror. Superiors? he queried. As in... military?

But no other clue emerged and, disgusted, Paul turned on the tap full force and doused his battered face with cold water.

The image of another soot-blackened face suddenly presented itself. Jane. Smoke. Turning off the water, Paul could smell it, suddenly.

Still frowning at his alien and disreputable self in the mirror, Paul brought an arm up to his nose. Sure enough, his skin reeked of smoke and he thought, Ah... So it hadn't all been a dream. There had been smoke, and a fire. And he really had searched for the woman. Anna. No, not Anna, Jane.

Jane. His... *wife?*

Concerned and confused, Paul slowly turned away from the sink and the mirror. He wondered, had he found her? And, if so, where was she? For that matter, where was *he?* There seemed to be no lingering traces of fire or smoke here in this place.

Still naked and too preoccupied to worry about it, Paul used walls and bits of furniture as supports while he made his unsteady way through the bedroom into the hall and beyond to a living room. He spared scarcely a glance for bright floral cushions and invitingly deep armchairs as his gaze homed in on the sleeping form on the sofa. Disheveled flaxen hair, a soot-smudged face, though no smile. Still, it was Jane.

Relief turned his already rubbery knees to jelly and he sank down on the wide arm of the nearest stuffed chair. He didn't know what he would have done if he hadn't found her. She was his anchor, his link to reality. Whatever he'd gone through, imagined or real, she had gone through it with him. Perhaps that was why, though he didn't remember her from before, he could nevertheless accept that she was his wife.

She simply felt like someone familiar, like someone he could trust to keep him safe until the key to his memory could be found.

Staring at her, he saw that her fine hair, too, was dusted with black. As was the hand that lay curled, childlike in sleep, beneath her chin. The stamp of exhaustion was on her face.

Tenderness stirred in him, and something like pride, too. It seemed she was a fighter, his Jane. She had fought for him and she had fought the fire. And somehow she had managed to get him here. He thought he remembered a car, heat, chills, an embrace. A kiss. Such a kiss!

Dreams? Reality? Whatever the case, it was all a foggy blur. He had been ill, but for how long? What day was this? Indeed, what year? A thousand questions crowded his mind, but a chill puckered his naked skin and caused him to shiver.

Quietly, so as not to wake the sleeping woman, Paul stood up. A hot shower, some clean clothes and then a look around to get his bearings, that was the ticket.

The steamy sting of the shower had the effect of a good massage on Paul's stiff-and-aching joints and muscles. He might not remember *how* he'd gotten himself tossed into the ocean, but it was obvious he had put up a good fight before being tossed back to shore.

There to be found—and rescued—by his own wife? Quite a coincidence.

Drying himself with the large fluffy bath sheet he had found in the cupboard beneath the sink, the thought gave him pause.

There had been a storm. He could remember the sound of rain pelting glass and wind shaking rafters the first time he'd awakened. Could he and Jane have gotten caught by the storm in a boat of some sort and been shipwrecked?

To be washed ashore in front of their own house? Hardly plausible. Besides, Jane said *she* had found *him* on the beach, in the surf. Meaning, she couldn't very well have been in the water with him, now could she?

Questions. Paul slammed down the towel and raked both hands through his damp hair. So many damned questions to which he had no answers. They were making his head feel as if it were splitting in two.

Women's things filled the dresser drawers and most of the closet. Just as he hadn't unearthed a razor in the bathroom, there was nothing of his here to wear. Which could only mean that he didn't ordinarily live in this place.

Did Jane?

Could it be they were . . . separated? Or divorced?

More questions. Paul muttered a curse. In Gorsk, he realized, surprised. Which was the same language in which a part of his thoughts randomly seemed to choose to express themselves. And now he knew the name of that language. Gorsk. From the country of Gorska.

Could it be that, little by little, pertinent information of his past was being restored to him?

His fingers tightening on the man's sweats he had unearthed in the back of the closet, he slowly straightened. His brow furrowed as he strained to recall other things. For instance, if he'd ever been to Gorska.

It was a small country in Central America, he knew that much. Yet he had no idea *how* he knew that, nor did he otherwise have any recollection of the place.

His stomach growled. He was hungry. Hungry and irritated, and frustrated as hell by the dead ends he encountered at every turn. Without bothering about
underwear, he got into the sweats and retraced his steps
to the living room. Jane still slept.

Something about chicken soup emerged from the fog
of his mind. Perhaps there was some waiting for him in
the kitchen. Which was where?

It didn't prove hard to find. Little more than a cubi-
cle, it was preceded by the small dining area off the living room and was as attractive and bright as everything
else seemed to be in this place. The entire apartment
struck Paul as miniature, however, making him feel like
Gulliver in Lilliput and reinforcing his conviction that
this was not his home.

He found himself hoping that it wasn't Jane's home,
either. That they weren't separated or divorced and that,
after the fire, Jane had simply brought him to the flat of
an absentee friend.

Of chicken soup there wasn't a trace. Paul's stomach
lamented that fact with another, protracted series of
rumbles. Mentally begging his unknown hostess's pardon for being so forward, he opened the refrigerator door
with every intention of finding sustenance.

The refrigerator's interior, however, gaped in gleaming emptiness. Only a jar of mayonnaise, some mustard,
tomato catsup and three cans of something that was
dauntingly labeled Diet Root Beer occupied the stain-
less-steel shelves. With a sinking feeling, Paul tried each
of the two drawers but, aside from a wilted lettuce leaf in
the one, there was nothing to eat there, either.

*"Donde!"* Paul disgustedly slammed the refrigerator
door and straightened. Didn't this woman believe in real
food?

He scanned the row of white-painted cupboards and opened one at random. Ah! Pay dirt of sorts. Some tins of, let's see now...black olives? Chili peppers? A jar of brownish goop labeled Peanut Butter. Who'd ever heard of such a thing?

Paul gingerly unscrewed the lid and sniffed. It smelled of peanuts, all right. With his stomach reminding him that peanuts were food, he scooped up a small portion with his finger and sucked it off. Hmm... Aside from the fact that the stuff made his tongue stick to the roof of his mouth, it wasn't bad. If all else failed, he'd find a spoon and— Ah.

His eyes lit on a familiar box—corn flakes. All was not lost. Except—Paul sighed and consoled himself with another scoop of peanut butter—there was no milk, of course.

Investigation of the other two cupboards did not yield anything a hungry man could sink his teeth into, either. He did spot a box of whole-wheat crackers and promptly ate some along with scoops of peanut butter. Munching, he wondered if anyone else realized what a tasty combination that was.

Apart from the crackers, there were two boxes of macaroni and cheese, three cans of tuna, some sugar, coffee. Decaffeinated?

Paul grimaced, appalled. Why bother with it, then? And lots of herbal tea. People subsisted on stuff like this? Paul shook his head. Incredible.

Cradling the box of crackers, he found a knife in the first drawer he opened and carried it, along with the jar of peanut butter, back into the living room.

"What're you doing?" Jane was awake and staring at him as if at an intruder.

Paul grinned, saluting her with the cracker box and thinking she looked delectable in her sleepy state, soot smudges and all. "Eating," he said, "as best I can."

"You've been snooping." What, besides peanut butter and crackers, had the man discovered about her?

"Guilty as charged." Paul pulled the chair away from an ornate little desk and, munching, sat down. "I was hungry."

Joy sat up on the sofa. "You're feeling better, then, I take it."

"Much." His smile was warm, intimate. "Thanks to you. Darling?" he hazarded. "Is that what I call you?"

"Um—" Joy felt relief at his question—he still had amnesia, thank God—but shock, too, as the enormity of her deception, as well as the myriad details and potential glitches with which she would have to contend, were brought home to her. "You, uh— No, not darling."

Vern had always called her his "li'l darlin'." She wouldn't want to hear something similar from Paul.

"What, then?" Paul asked, his gaze so intense, Joy had to look away.

"Do we have to talk of this now?" she said, standing up and busying herself with fluffing the cushions she had crushed during sleep. Flustered—she had a sudden, and very vivid, recollection of his naked physique—she mumbled the first thing that came to mind. "I must look a mess."

"Ah, but charmingly so," Paul said gallantly, drawing Joy's gaze back to his. "Still, perhaps a shower and some food . . . ?"

He was looking at her as if he knew her, Joy thought, unable to break eye contact yet increasingly unsettled by the warm lights that glowed in his. As if he owned her. As if he were pleased to know she was his.

"Try some of these crackers with peanut butter," he said. "You might think it a strange combination—I did— but it's really quite good. And there isn't much else in the way of food in this place, I'm afraid."

*Peanut butter and crackers, strange?* Joy stared at him and thought, Did people forget about everyday foods, too, when they suffered amnesia? Somehow she doubted it. And she wondered again, Who *was* this man? And where did he come from?

A renewed sense of unease tied her stomach in knots. "No, thank you," she managed when he held out a cracker. "I couldn't. I, uh, I'm not hungry."

A lengthening silence fell between them. They continued to contemplate each other, but their expressions had become mutually guarded. Neither could read the other, neither was at ease.

"This isn't our home, is it?" Paul asked at length. His tone was level, only lightly tinged with curiosity.

Joy closed her eyes and mentally braced herself. The way not to trip herself up, she reasoned, was to stick as much as possible to the truth.

So, was this *their* home? No. It was hers. Alone.

She took a deep breath, swallowed and shook her head. "No."

"Oh, good." Paul's smile made Joy's knees go weak. "I was afraid I might have forgotten some antifood cult or something that we belong to."

Joy laughed, weakly.

"What kinds of clubs or *cults*—" he winked "—do we belong to? Any I should know about?"

"No. That is—" Help, I'm not very good at this. "We, uh, we don't belong to any, um, to anything . . . like that or . . . anything."

Studying her, observing her obvious nervousness with him, Paul pursed his lips. "We haven't been married for very long, have we, *carsya?*"

"Uh." Joy shook her head. "No."

Increasingly discomfited by Paul's close and intimate scrutiny, Joy thought, a little hysterically, What am I doing? I can't do this. And then, with sudden resolve, I'm going to tell him.

She began, "As a matter of fact—"

"There's a calendar here on this desk." His mind still occupied with learning personal statistics, Paul unthinkingly interrupted. "It says April third. Is that today?"

"No," Joy said impatiently, "today's Easter Sunday. But—" She was eager to get on with her confession before she lost her nerve. "Paul, there's something I have to te—"

She broke off as something clicked. Easter Sunday?

"Oh my gosh!" Suddenly frantic, she squeezed by Paul to the desk. With trembling fingers she flipped the pages of the daily calendar until she came to April twelfth. Sure enough—Easter Sunday.

Her eyes wild, she spun around. "What time is it?"

Paul, with no idea, gazed at her in consternation. Was it something he'd said?

"Almost ten," Joy gasped with a horrified glance at the clock. "Ma expected me for church half an hour ago. She'll be sending out a posse if I don't get a hold of her. Excuse me."

She reached past Paul to the phone and punched out her mother's number. While she waited for her mother to answer, gazing at the ceiling and tapping her foot, Paul got up off the chair and walked away from the desk.

Her anxious voice stopped him.

"Where're you going?"

ANNE PETERS61

Half turning, he gestured in the direction of the window. "Nowhere. I only thought I'd..."

"Never mind." Joy slammed down the phone. With Paul trailing behind, she rushed to the bedroom, talking all the way. "Ma's gone. Looking for me, I'll bet. She knows I'm back from Seattle—"

"Seattle?"

"It's a long story." Joy barely broke stride, her mind in three directions at once. "Anyway, she always worries about me staying alone at the beach house—"

"The beach house?"

"Where we had the chimney fire." She stopped in front of her dresser and faced Paul. "You do remember the chimney fire?"

Smoke, thick and black. Paul nodded. "Ah, yes, I believe I—"

"Good." Joy yanked open a drawer and rummaged around. "I think," she muttered to herself.

Aloud she said, "In any case, once Ma gets a load of the place and sees my car is gone, she'll be over here lickety-split. So here's what we'd better do. You go to the window and keep a lookout while I grab a quick shower. When you see them pull up in front of the house, call and I'll head 'em off at the pass. Okay?"

Slamming drawers and gathering fresh underwear, Joy caught sight of Paul's bemused expression. She straightened, feeling bad. "I'm going way too fast for you, aren't I?"

"You might say that, yes." Truth was, Paul's head was reeling from everything he'd heard. Only little of which made sense.

"I'm sorry," Joy said sincerely. She could see how confused he was and wished she could take the time to fill him in. "It's all my fault," she said. "And I wanted to explain it to you, I really did. But now—" She tossed up her hands. "I'm sorry, Paul. There just isn't time."

A glance at the bedside clock made it clear just how little time there was.

Joy switched gears, her tone once again breathless with urgency. "Please, Paul, play along with me? I know it's confusing and I'll explain it all later, but, for now, can you just trust me?"

"How can I not?" Paul said, and his expression seared Joy to her very soul. "Jane. You're all there is for me right now."

"Oh, Paul." Tears rushed to Joy's eyes. She felt like dirt, but knew there wasn't time to indulge in guilt trips.

"Please go to the window," she said and closed the bathroom door in his face.

Staring at it, Paul shook his head. He wasn't sure *what* was going on, but was convinced that *something* was. Something that involved him, but in ways about which he had no idea. She was cooking something up, that wife of his, but he hadn't a clue as to what. He intended to find out, though. But first, there was a street to be watched for arriving cars.

With a last, lingering look at the bathroom door from behind which the rush of shower water could be heard, he reluctantly turned away and walked out of the bedroom.

He had just set foot in the hall when the chime of the doorbell arrested his step. It was followed immediately by a loud and insistent pounding on the door above which agitated voices could be heard. And then the scratching of a key in the lock.

Paul called out, "Jane!" and had just reached for the handle when the door swung forcefully toward him.

He stepped aside and barely avoided being trampled as two giant Vikings barged into the apartment. A slight, graying but still youthful woman followed in their wake.

Paul stood quietly next to the bedroom door, but the sight of him instantly arrested everyone's movement. For several heartbeats, they stared at him and he stared at them.

And then the larger of the two Vikings lunged at Paul and grabbed a fistful of his shirt. "And just who the hell," he growled, "are you?"

# Chapter Five

"Ernest Cooper, you let go of him right now!"
Wrapped in a bath sheet and with her hair dripping, Joy
burst onto the scene.

Paul, still trapped by the blond giant's stranglehold on
his shirt, and nose-to-nose with Jane's fire-breathing
brother—other than size, the family resemblance was
startling—wished Jane had taken time to get dressed. So,
apparently, did her family.

"Daughter, you go and get decent this instant!" her
mother exclaimed, aghast, as Jane's brother growled,
"Stay outta this, sis, 'n' get your clothes on."

Since they obviously didn't know who he was, and in
view of the shortness of everyone's fuses, Paul thought
some explanations might restore order. After all, things
weren't what they might appear to be. He and Jane were
married.

"This isn't—" he began, but a twist of the brother's
fist on his shirt cut off his air and his speech.

Joy ignored the lot of them. She was furious with her brother's strong-arm tactics which, more often than not, had always been the way he had dealt with any situation involving her, the baby sister.

"I said, let him go," she seethed from between clenched teeth and, when her brother merely glared at her without complying, calmly took hold of his arm and bit it.

"Hell's bells, sissy." Wincing, Ernest turned Paul loose. "You promised not to bite me anymore."

"I lied." Joy glared at him, one hand clutching the towel at her breast to keep it from slipping. "Just as it seems like you lied about not interfering in my life anymore."

Dismissing her brother who was scowling and rubbing his abused arm, her expression became contrite as she turned to her mother. "I'm sorry, Ma, for worrying you. As soon as I realized what day and time it was, I tried to call, but—"

Spreading her hands in a gesture of helplessness, she fell silent. She realized this wasn't the time to blurt out everything, especially since she wasn't sure just how much of that "everything" she should spill.

It was obvious that the news of her "marriage" had not yet reached their ears. No doubt that would change after church today. So she needed to do some thinking— fast. But for that she needed time alone.

"Look," she suggested, "whyn't you all go into the living room while I go get dressed and Paul here grabs a—"

She broke off, glancing at Paul. She had meant to say "grabs a shower," but he had already done that, of course. She noted with a pang of guilt that he was very pale beneath the bruises and stubble. He was built so strongly, and had earlier seemed so...recovered, she had momentarily lost sight of his fragile state of health.

Poor guy, she thought. Talk about being tossed from the frying pan into the fire! After all he'd been through, this set-to with Ernie and the rest of the family was the last thing he needed.

"Paul needs a shave," she said firmly and, taking Paul by the arm, pulled him into the bedroom.

Behind them, hell broke lose all over again, with her mother and Ernie shouting at once.

Joy stilled the babble with a shrill, two-finger whistle. "Everybody, into the living room."

She grabbed her brother around the middle and forcibly turned him around. "All I ask for is fifteen minutes of peace and then I'll explain everything."

"But—" her mother said, only to have Joy hush her with a quick hug and kiss.

"Fifteen minutes, Ma. Okay?"

In the bedroom, Joy subsided against the door with her eyes squeezed shut. Her knees knocked. "Phew."

"Jane."

Oh, gosh, *Paul*. She didn't have it in her to explain anything to him right now. Not after the fiasco in the hall moments before.

But he gave her no choice. He stepped right up to her, so close, the heat of his body wrapped around her like a cocoon.

"Jane." His voice was low but vibrating with tension

Reluctantly, Joy opened her eyes. His face was set.

"Your family doesn't know me, Jane. They don't know of me. I think that some explanations are in order."

"Now?" All her eagerness to confess had fallen by the wayside. "It's a long story," she prevaricated, and the words sounded lame even to her own ears. "We've only got about ten minutes—"

"Then you'd better talk fast, hadn't you?" Paul folded his arms and raised his brows. "Are you and I married?"

Put on the spot, without time to reason things out, Joy flared, "Would I tell you we were if we weren't?"

Paul eyed her thoughtfully for—it seemed to Joy—uncomfortably long moments during which she was hard put to keep her eyes level on his. "I don't know," he finally said. "Would you?"

Joy blinked. More than anything, she wanted to look away. But to do so would make her seem guilty and she couldn't afford that now. She had been caught by her family, scantily clad and with a man in her bedroom. The die had been cast.

"What do *you* think?" she blustered.

"I don't know." Paul rubbed his chin, and his prolonged contemplation made Joy sweat bullets. "It seems every one of your answers gives rise to more questions. But all right, when was the wedding?"

"Um..." Joy briefly considered pretending not to understand, but then thought better of it. She could hardly hope to convince her family she was married to Paul without first telling him at least *something* of the supposed circumstances leading up to it.

Closing her eyes—his intent regard made it so darned difficult to lie—she swallowed. "We, uh— It was an act of impulse. A, you know...a lark—"

"When?"

Joy took a deep breath and crossed her fingers. "A few days ago. I—"

"We eloped?"

Joy hung her head. "Well, yes. Sort of..."

Paul put a finger beneath her chin and raised it. "Look at me, Jane."

"Joy."

"Pardon?"

Taking advantage of Paul's consternation, Joy ducked beneath his arm to relative freedom. Or, at least, breathing space.

"My name is Joy," she said. "I've no idea why you keep calling me Jane."

"Because you told me..."

"I most certainly did not." Joy marched to the dresser and picked up her hairbrush. "My name is Joy. Joy Marie. Why would I tell you it's Jane?"

"I've no idea."

Paul watched, riveted, as Joy bent from the waist and vigorously brushed her, by now, almost dry hair. One hand clutched the towel she had wrapped around herself like a sarong, but even so, a good bit of delectable skin was bared for his enjoyment. Such fair, creamy skin. His fingers itched to touch it.

"Tell me, Joy Marie," he said. "Are you in love with me?"

"What!" Joy whiplashed upright and stared at him. "Now what kind of a fool question is that?"

"Quite a relevant one." Paul came close and indulged himself by trailing a finger across the smooth skin of her shoulder. It was velvet and silk, heaven to touch. "If, as you say, we are married."

Catching her unawares, he put his arms around her and pulled her close. So close, their bodies touched. Joy was too surprised to even think of resisting.

"Answer me, Joy." He tugged and brought her closer, until her body was in intimate contact with his.

A jolt of heat made Joy tremble. As she felt a similar reaction in Paul, her mouth went dry.

"I . . . c-could ask y-you the same thing," she whispered haltingly, her voice rough and uneven. "And what would you say?"

"That I'm not sure." Paul's gaze, dropping to her lips, kindled. "I *am* sure, however, that I want you, *carsya mu*. Desperately. And since we are married . . ."

His eyes, bright with the fevered light Joy had seen in them before. He lowered his head. And before Joy could do anything more than blink, he closed the small gap between them and his mouth, moist and open, settled hotly on hers. Devoured hers.

"Paul—" *Not now,* Joy started to protest, but found herself helpless in the face of his passionate assault. But no, not helpless. First boneless. Then compliant. And then eagerly melting and greedy for more.

She fastened her arms around Paul's waist and clung to his strength. For although he trembled as violently as she, she knew it wasn't from weakness, but from the same desperate need that held her enthralled, erasing reason and thought.

Paul shifted his stance, moved his hips, slanted his mouth across Joy's in a desperate attempt to make her fully a part of himself. To make her fill the void of his lost memory and make him whole.

And Joy followed, moaned, accommodated. Aware of nothing but Paul's lips, Paul's hands, Paul's iron-hard form, she reveled in his heat, his need, his all-consuming desire and responded in kind. Wildly, greedily, mindlessly, the way she had never responded to any man before.

Vaguely, she felt herself lifted off her feet and swung up into strong arms. Her arms encircled his neck, her towel came undone and half slipped to the floor. And still their kiss went on.

*"Trusora,"* Paul growled against her lips, into her mouth. "You're my wife. I need you. Want you. Say it, *eposa mu.* Say that you want me, too."

"Yes..." Joy kissed him wildly, holding tight. Nothing else mattered. Time had ceased to be. No one existed but Paul. "Oh my God, yes..."

"What the hell?" The bedroom door hit the wall with a reverberating crash and Ernest Cooper's massive form filled the opening.

With a muttered curse, Paul pressed his forehead to Joy's. He struggled for breath, for sanity. When at last he was able, he raised his head and glared at the intruder.

"I am kissing my wife," he snarled. "Do you—?"

*Mind,* he'd been going to say.

But Joy, crying, *"No!"* belatedly clapped a hand over his mouth.

Her gaze skidded from Paul's shocked expression to the outrage in her brother's eyes. "Please put me down," she said to Paul, and at the last second clutched at the towel before it fell off her completely.

"Get dressed," Paul ordered in a tone of such possessive command that Joy, as well as Ernie, shot him a look of surprise.

Without a word, Joy went into the bathroom and slipped into her thick terry robe. It buttoned down the front and covered her from neck to toe. Decent enough for an audience with the Pope, she thought, and, head high, walked back into the bedroom.

She was amazed by how calm she felt now that the moment she had dreaded was at hand. Thanks to Paul, Ernie knew now that she was married. And maybe that was just as well. She had never been very good at premeditated lies. Perhaps winging it without time to consider the consequences would be best all around.

Deep breath. Oh, Lord, this was hard. She summoned a smile, but it instantly faltered when she caught sight of her mother, and brother Dennis, too, hovering behind Ernie in the doorway.

"*He* says they're married." Ernie, narrow-eyed and visibly primed for a fight, sent a scathing glare in Paul's direction.

Paul returned the stare with nostrils flared and head high.

They reminded Joy of two roosters squaring off in the chicken yard, and she might have found them amusing, had not her mother's distressed cry of "Married?" assaulted her like the slap of a hand.

"Just like that?" her mother exclaimed in shocked tones. "Without a word to anyone? To me?"

Joy swallowed a lump of guilt and dismay. The entire scene was so much more traumatic than she'd ever thought it would be.

Thought? She did a mental double-take, telling herself that that was the trouble, wasn't it? She *hadn't* thought before starting all this.

Feeling cornered, she became defensive. "For heaven's sake, Ma, I'm twenty-six years old. I surely don't need—"

"Need? No," her mother cut in, her tone aggrieved. "But I would have thought you'd have wanted to, Joy Marie."

Her mother's hurt expression made Joy feel smaller than a gnat. Needing to lash out, she rounded on her brother. "You!" she cried. "This is all your fault. Who're you to barge in here when I told you to wait? When I said I'd explain...."

"So explain."

"Could I possibly get dressed first? In private?" Joy added pointedly when nobody made a move to leave the room.

Brother Dennis, a fisherman who never said much and who until now had been characteristically silent, suddenly spoke up. "What about church?" he said. "Marje, Jolene an' the kids'll be expecting us."

"Good thinking, Den." Joy was ready to jump on any bandwagon that might convey her family out of her apartment. And herself out of this predicament, even if only for a little while.

"Why don't you three go ahead on to church? Please?" she added in the face of their obvious reluctance. Her head was pounding and she very badly needed a breather from this cloak-and-dagger drama in which she had so foolhardily cast herself as the lead. "Paul and I'll catch up with you at the house for the egg hunt and Easter dinner."

Marie Cooper turned to her sons. "You boys go ahead downstairs and wait for me in the car. I'll be right down. Joy," she said to her daughter, "I'd like a word with you. Alone.

"Excuse us," she said to Paul and left the bedroom in her sons' wake, clearly expecting Joy to follow.

With a pained glance of apology to Paul, Joy did.

Her mother was at the living room window. Joy went to stand beside her. For a moment, neither spoke. They saw Dennis and Ernie emerge from the house and head for the full-size aging sedan that was Marie Cooper's transportation of choice. She could well have afforded a newer, smaller automobile, but this one had been bought by her husband, it was reliable and she cherished it.

"Why, Joy?" Marie finally said. "You're my only daughter. Can you blame me if I want to be part of something as important as planning your wedding?"

"You already did that once, Ma," Joy said quietly, referring to her wedding plans with Vernon Harris that had so precipitously come to naught. "Remember? We did it all, you and I—the gown, the invitations, the cake..."

Her voice steadily rising in agitation, she spoke faster and faster. "...the church, the bridesmaids, flowers. We did it all, Ma. Remember? Even the gosh-darned thank-you notes!"

Joy buried her face in her hands.

"Baby, I'm sorry." Marie took Joy by the shoulders and gently turned her so they faced each other. "Look at me. Please."

Reluctantly, Joy lowered her hands. Her mother's concerned gaze was both a balm and an irritant. Pity— how she loathed being the recipient of it. Weakness—how she hated to give in to it.

"All I want," Marie said, "is your happiness. Are you happy? Will you tell me that?"

"Oh, Ma. I'm happier than I've been in a long time." And Joy realized that, incredibly, it was the truth.

"Very well." Her mother smiled, misty-eyed. "You'll hear no more I-wish-you-had's from me, then." She squeezed Joy's hands. "All right?"

Swallowing the tears that had pooled, unshed, in her throat, Joy managed a smile. "All right."

"But tell me," her mother said, "who is this husband of yours?"

"His name is Paul Mallik."

"Mallik. Where . . . ?"

"I, uh, knew him back in college," Joy said, withdrawing her hands from her mother's so she could cross her fingers at the lie.

In spite of her mother's tacit acceptance of the status quo, Joy knew very well she wouldn't leave without further explanations. Other families might take a lighter view of a situation such as this, or even come to verbal blows and part in anger. Not so the Coopers. Differences or problems were neither ignored nor battled over for long. They were discussed, and they were settled.

"From the UW, in Seattle."

"I remember quite well where you went to college, Joy Marie. So, you kept in touch all this time?"

"No." Too restless and guilt-stricken to stand still, Joy began to pace. "We, uh, sort of ran into each other when I went back there after Vernon . . ."

"After Vernon . . ." Marie repeated pensively.

"Yes. Well, it seems Paul's been, uh, carrying a torch for me all these years. . . ."

"How romantic."

Sarcasm? From her mother? Joy sent her a quick sideways glance, but could read nothing in her mother's expression.

"We partied," she said, frantically searching for something that would make marriage sound plausible. "One thing led to another and . . ."

With a helpless shrug, Joy let the sentence, and what it implied, hang.

"And so you got married," her mother said.

Joy let silence be her answer. She stood at her desk, her back to her mother. Cracker crumbs littered the blotter from Paul's—to him—unlikely meal.

Paul. Joy raised a fist to her mouth and bit down on it. What was she doing to him with this charade?

"Do you love him?" her mother asked from right behind her.

Joy closed her eyes. "I—"

"No, don't answer that. I think I already know. It's because of Vern, isn't it?"

Full of sudden fury, Joy spun around. "Well what if it is?" She flung her arms wide, crying, "Vernon Harris dumped me two days before my wedding and the whole town went, Poor Joy Marie! She lost her man.

"Well, Joy Marie went and found herself another man. A better man..."

"Is he?" Marie caught Joy's flailing hands and held them fast. "Is he a better man?"

"Yes!" Joy pulled free one of her hands and angrily swiped at the flood of tears swamping her face. "Paul's crazy about me. He wants me. Needs me..."

"And you, baby?"

"Oh, Ma!" With a sob, Joy flung herself into her mother's arms. "All I want is for somebody to want me. Is that so wrong?"

"No, baby, that isn't wrong." Teary-eyed herself, Marie Cooper stroked her daughter's back. "That's only being human."

But even as she spoke the words that were meant to soothe and reassure her distraught daughter, Marie's gaze met the blazing eyes of her new son-in-law across the room. And she wondered, Had she said the right thing?

* * *

"So I'm only a stand-in husband, is that it?"

Paul had heard every word of Joy's exchange with her mother and knew a devastating sense of betrayal. He marveled how steady his voice was when inside he trembled and shook with outrage and—yes, dammit—pain. "Am I a means to an end?"

Marie Cooper had departed moments earlier, leaving him alone with Joy.

She had dried her tears and looked utterly miserable.

In fact, Joy was more than miserable. She was filled with self-loathing. Admitting her self-serving motives aloud had shamed her in ways she had never before been shamed.

But facing Paul, witnessing his disillusionment was infinitely worse yet. He thought they were married. And the motives she had confessed to her mother had hurt him deeply.

She *had* to tell him the truth.

"I'm sorry," she said, and didn't need Paul's disdainful snort to remind her how inadequate that apology was. "It's not the way you think."

"Really." Paul wandered over to the window and blindly stared out. "And how is it?"

"We, uh . . . We're not . . ." Oh, Lord, this was hard. But if to no one else, to Paul she owed the truth.

"We're not really married."

There, it was out. A weight dropped off Joy's shoulders. But one glance at the face Paul slowly turned toward her, had that weight settling instead with a sickening lurch in the pit of her stomach.

He was angry.

*Angry* was putting it mildly. Paul was thunderstruck. And he was livid. But most of all, incredibly, he was disappointed.

In the short time since his rescue, Joy had been such a warm and caring constant, he had *liked* thinking of her as his. As his wife.

She had been the only reality when everything else in his present and past had been reduced to bewildering, formless and murky shapes. He had told himself that whatever follies he might have committed in his nebulous past, at least he'd had the good sense to choose a lovable and loving mate.

But he hadn't, had he? Nor was Joy a loving wife. It was all a lie, an act. Everything? The caring, the warmth? The rescue?

*Donde!* What else hadn't she told him?

"Who am I?" he demanded, his tone as carefully neutral as his emotions now were. Somewhere he must have learned to compartmentalize his feelings, to effectively shut them down. He was grateful now for the lessons. "You know, don't you?"

"No." Joy shook her head, sick at heart. How hard he seemed, how implacable. The passionate man, the vulnerable stranger—both were gone. "All I know is what you yourself told me. Your name is Paul."

"Paul." Saying it brought no echo of recognition.

"And I think your last name is Mallik," Joy said. She spelled it. "*M-A-L-L-I-K.* That was stitched on the wet suit you had on."

"A wet suit."

Thinking it a question, Joy said, "You know, what divers—"

Paul cut her off with a glare. "I know what a wet suit is."

*Divers.* The word struck a chord in him that hummed in his brain like a familiar tune. A picture formed on his mental screen, one he immediately recognized as a diving bell.

He closed his eyes. For a moment it seemed the floor beneath his feet undulated like the deck of a ship. Gales howled. Water. Churning, riotous water was everywhere.

With a choked sound of distress, Paul covered his eyes. He stumbled, and might have fallen, had Joy not rushed over and steadied him.

"Paul," she cried, concern for him overriding every other emotion. "Oh, Paul, what is it?"

She put an arm around him and led him to the couch. She urged him down on it. "Let me get you some water."

Water. A ship.

Paul let his pounding head drop back against the backrest of the sofa. He wanted to remember. If only he could remember....

"Here." Joy held the glass to his lips. "Drink this."

Paul took a sip, coughed and spluttered. His eyes flew open. "This isn't water."

"No. It's brandy." Joy anxiously scanned his face. His color was better, but not much. "Here." She urged the glass back to his mouth. "Take another sip. It'll do you good."

Paul took the small glass from her hand and tossed its contents back with one twist of the wrist. As the brandy warmed its way down to his stomach, soothing and smoothing some of the knots there as it went, his emotions, too, once again stirred to life. He contemplated Joy's worried expression with hooded eyes.

"My Good Samaritan," he murmured. "I suppose, everything considered, I owe you a huge debt of gratitude."

"You owe me nothing," Joy said vehemently. She took the glass he held out to her and found her hand captured by his.

"Nothing?" he asked with a quizzical half smile. "Isn't your mother expecting you and *your husband* for an egg hunt and Easter dinner?"

"Yes, well." Flustered by the change in him, Joy tugged on her hand. "I'll go alone and explain. . . ."

"What? That you lied to them? That we aren't really married?"

"Yes." Joy tugged again and this time Paul released her. "This whole thing has gotten out of hand. I never intended—"

"Just what *did* you intend?"

"Not this," Joy said bitterly. She looked down at the shot glass in her hand, twisted it round and round. "Not this snowballing of lies. People getting hurt. You, Ma..."

She half turned her head and met his gaze. "Believe me, I never meant for any of that to happen."

"Perhaps I'm a fool, but I do believe you." Paul rose from the sofa and gently touched her face where traces of tears still lingered. "And that's why I think there is time enough for the truth later, when the Easter celebrations are past. Don't you think?"

Joy stared at him. Where his finger touched her face, her skin tingled. She longed to tell him...what? So many things, and yet there was nothing she could say. Even had the right to say.

For who knew the man he really was? Surely, he belonged somewhere. To someone.

She bit her lip. Unbidden, tears stung her eyes. "Do you mean . . . ?"

"That I'll play the role of your husband till you figure out a way to tell your family the truth, yes."

His thumb brushed her lips, which, at his words, had begun to curve into a watery smile of thanks. "They all love you very much, you know. Even—or maybe especially—that ferocious big brother of yours."

Using the chimney fire in the beach house as an excuse for Paul's lack of appropriate clothing, Joy, dressed in a pink suit, cream-colored blouse and spectator pumps, and Paul in sweats, presented themselves at Marie Cooper's weathered North-Coast-style house in Seacrest.

Mercifully, the brothers and their families had not yet arrived

Marie greeted Paul with matter-of-fact cordiality. Joy was hugged and kissed. Not a word was said about the events of the morning.

Within minutes of their arrival, explaining that their family always dressed up for Easter and she wouldn't want him to feel out of place, Marie was urging Paul into a surprisingly well-fitting suit of clothes.

"They were my husband's," she explained, checking Paul over with obvious pleasure after he had—admittedly with initial reluctance—put everything on. "He died at sea, God rest him. His boat went down with all hands."

Her eyes clouded for a moment, betraying to Paul that she still grieved the loss. But then she took a deep breath and blustered, much like Joy was prone to doing, "Lord knows why I hang on to his stuff. It's been ten years and there's surely no chance..."

She waved the rest of the sentence away with a frown of impatience. "How're the shoes?"

Paul had looked down at the cordovan dress shoes and decided to be honest. "Ouch."

They both laughed then, which was when Joy came into the room. She went quite still and white at the sight of him.

"That's Pop's," she said, her eyes clouding the way her mother's had. Mr. Cooper was a lucky man, Paul thought with a pang, to be mourned this deeply for so long.

For the first time since he had regained consciousness, it occurred to him to wonder if there might be someone mourning *him*. Until now, with all that had happened, he hadn't stopped to think of family, of friends or of a... wife?

And he realized that he would have to find out. More, that he owed it to himself and to those unremembered loved ones to get well as soon as possible while, in the meantime, making every effort to uncover his true identity.

The situation as it was could not go on. Tomorrow he would seek out the sheriff and a doctor and start the ball rolling.

Joy was still looking at him, her eyes misty with nostalgia, but with something else, too. Something that struck a responding chord in Paul and, in spite of all that had transpired, and in spite of everything he'd just been thinking, made awareness hum between them again.

"You look wonderful," Joy said, the breathy quality in her voice hinting at a heart beating faster, just as his had begun to do.

Paul knew then that there was no use in denying it, or in wishing it weren't so. The fact was, she made him feel something, this Good Samaritan of his. Husbandly? Maybe. Loverlike? Oh, yes.

But the question was, without knowing his past, without knowing what commitments he might have made, or what ties bound him there, did he have the right to feel anything but gratitude for Joy Marie Cooper?

Everyone had already assembled in the spacious backyard when Paul and Joy came outside. Ernie and Dennis Cooper's wives were called Marjorie and Jolene. They didn't seem to share their husband's reticence.

Jolene Cooper was as jolly as her name implied, in contrast to her husband, Ernie, who couldn't seem to stop scowling. Especially when looking at Joy or Paul.

He's not buying his sister's story, Paul thought uneasily. Still, the man's acuity impressed as much as distressed him. No fool, was Ernest Cooper. But considerate enough to leave well enough alone for now and not to spoil the holiday.

Dennis was a more amiable fellow, at least in his outward demeanor. He was a silent one, however, content to sit and listen while the conversation ebbed and flowed around him. Paul had been told that Dennis was five years younger than Ernie, and that Joy, in turn, was another five years below Den. Father of two rambunctious boys who only turned shy when Paul talked to them, Dennis was doing his quiet best to put that morning's unpleasantness behind them just as his mother was.

Now he beckoned for Paul to join him and the others over by a vine-covered gazebo. "Best place to watch the show is from here," he said shyly, with a glance toward Joy.

She had the two boys—eight and ten—as well as Ernie's brood of three, standing with baskets in hand at an imaginary starting line. A whistle was poised to blow at her lips. Her myriad problems shelved for the moment, Joy's cheeks were flushed and her eyes sparkled. Her suit jacket had long since been shed along with her pumps. To Paul, she looked fetchingly disheveled with one tail of her cream silk shirt hanging out and with her feet in a pair of tattered sneakers.

Paul took a seat next to Dennis on the gazebo bench. "What are they waiting for?"

"Oh, Jolene's gone to get the youngsters from next door," Dennis's wife, Marjorie, said, leaning forward with a warm smile. "The more the merrier, as they say."

"Ah."

Moments later, with the neighbor kids having arrived with their parents in tow, Joy blew the whistle and, with a whoop and a holler, the hunt was on.

Clapping her hands with glee, clearly wishing she could be a participant instead of a mere observer and referee, Joy followed along while the neighbors joined the other adults in the gazebo.

Marie came from the house with mugs of coffee for everybody. Dinner was scheduled for later in the day. Paul was quick to go meet her and take the heavy tray from her hands.

"Why, thank you, Paul," said Marie with a loaded glance at her sons who had made no move to assist her. "Aren't you nice."

Paul met the Cooper men's sour expressions with a rueful one that implied, No harm in buttering up my new mother-in-law. Being married males, they could identify with that and, Dennis's brow at least, cleared.

While Paul held the tray, Marie handed out the steaming mugs. "Have you met the Garwoods, Paul?"

Paul, with a smile at the couple who lived near Marie, shook his head.

"Well, my goodness," Marie said, fussing at her sons. "Where're you boys' manners, anyway?"

She took the empty tray out of Paul's hands, set it down and drew him toward the newcomers. "Paul Mallik, meet Will and Debbie Garwood."

Smiles were exchanged and the men shook hands. "Mallik, eh?" Will Garwood scratched his balding pate. "Now, why's that name ring a bell?"

Shock made Paul's breath get stuck in his throat. This man knew him? Or, at least, he knew what Joy thought was his family name?

Paul's smile froze on his face. His entire body tensed as he waited for the other man to go on.

"Mallik...Mallik... Funny thing about me," Garwood said. "I never forget a name. Gimme a minute."

While Will Garwood ruminated, every nerve in Paul's body quivered with tension.

"Let's see now," Will muttered, his forefinger tapping his nose. "Seems like I read it somewheres. That's it. Yes!"

Garwood looked around in triumph. "It was in today's paper. In the Astoria *Trib!*"

At his exclamation, conversation stopped among the others and Garwood turned to include them. "Seems like one of them *U*nited Nations vessels took to port because

one of her officers—they're multinational, you know—
fell off the damned thing during the storm. Which makes
it what they call an *incident*," he explained importantly
while the world began to spin around Paul, "when one
of them foreigners goes overboard in American waters."

Garwood beamed at Paul, who was barely able to see
him through the swirling fog that had engulfed him.
Vaguely, he was aware that Joy had stopped playing with
the children and stood, listening, at the foot of the two
gazebo steps. Garwood's voice came from a distance,
echoing as through a tunnel.

"There's even a picture o' the man," he said.
"Damned if he isn't your spittin' image, too."

# Chapter Six

"Deb," Will Garwood said to his wife. "Run home and fetch me the *Trib,* will you, hon?"

Paul shook his head at the speed with which it was all happening. Like a movie on fast forward. He, his senses, were being bombarded by events, thoughts and images that included the immediate as well as the past. His mouth went as dry as the desert and he couldn't speak.

*Pavel Mallik. Pavel, Pavel,* not Paul. *Pavel Mallik.* Through the whirling maelstrom of his mind, the name chanted like a litany. Everything around him receded. He feared he would pass out. His eyes searched frantically for Joy and found her, gazing up at him with an expression that was a mixture of trepidation, hope and bewilderment.

As from the start, now, too, her mere presence served to anchor and steady him.

"I'm sorry." His lips formed the apology soundlessly. The last thing he would have wanted was to cause Joy more problems. Given a choice, he would have picked a more suitable time and place to regain his memory. But no choice had been given him.

"Don't bother, Mrs. Garwood," he said, surprised that his voice could sound so calm and firm when he felt as though he could barely stay upright. His eyes clung to Joy's as to a lifeline.

"I *am* the man whose picture is in the paper. I am Lt. Commander Pavel Mallik of the Gorskan navy on assignment to the U.N. research vessel *Explorer II*."

Joy's gasp, though visible to Paul, was inaudible. Or, Paul thought, still feeling curiously detached and light-headed, maybe her exclamation of shock and distress had merely been drowned out by her brother Ernie's infuriated bellow.

"Mister," Ernest Cooper barked, advancing on Paul like a maddened bull, "I want to have a word with you."

"Sorry." Paul's light-headedness increased. "Maybe...later...."

He tried to smile, tried to turn and apologize to Joy's mother for disrupting her gathering, but managed to do neither. The world spun around him, fast and faster. The ground dropped away from beneath his feet.

And then he was hurled into a black and nameless void where the awareness of his past and present crashed down on him with all the force of that gigantic wall of water that had swept him off his ship.

Paul came to in yet another strange bed. It seemed to him that made three in two days.

*Good things come in threes.* His mother used to say that to him as a boy.

His mother. All British bustle and propriety on the outside, but on the inside as soft and sweet as a squishy jelly bun. He had loved her. He still missed her. Much more than he had loved and missed his stern Gorskan career diplomat of a father.

Long dead now, both of them. As were Anna and Miguel . . .

With a mental wince, Paul slammed the door on that particular memory. Some things one was better off to forget.

Still, it was good to be back in his own skin, his own mind and body. For what was the body but an extension of the mind? Without that mind, without all the knowledge, the history, the memories that made up and shaped a man's personality and character, who was that man but an empty shell?

Well, Paul thought with a touch of wryness, he was empty no more.

The events leading up to this latest awakening in a strange bed rushed back to mind. Regret filled him. He would have preferred to spare Joy from finding out about him this way. In front of her family who thought he was her husband.

The door opened. As if called there by his thoughts, Joy walked into the room. Her face was pale, her expression grave. She carried a small glass half-filled with amber liquid.

"More brandy?" Paul queried, startling Joy into nearly spilling the stuff.

"Paul." She spoke his name like a soft caress and, for an instant, her expression crumbled as if she wanted to cry. "You gave us quite a turn."

But then she had herself back in hand. "I'm glad to see you're back among the living, Paul." She faltered. "I mean, Pavel, or—"

"Paul."

She stared at him. "But you said—"

"Pavel is the Gorskan version of Paul," Paul explained. "And Paul is the name my English mother always called me."

He hauled himself into a sitting position and scrubbed a hand across his face. "Funny I should have remembered that even when everything else was a blank."

"You remembered her language, too," Joy reminded him, handing him the glass. "And a good thing. I'm lousy at foreign languages."

"But very good with foreigners," Paul said warmly.

"Oh, you," Joy said, flustered. She pointed to the brandy. "Better drink that, it'll make you feel better."

Paul glanced at the glass in his hand and back at Joy with a droll expression. "If you insist on plying me with brandy, I shall probably soon feel a good deal worse."

Because their eye contact grew disturbingly long, and because he knew the attraction he felt could never lead to anything—he'd have to be back aboard ship just as soon as he could get himself there—he glanced around.

"This was your room, wasn't it?"

"Yes." Unnerved by Paul in a strange new way, Joy followed his gaze.

"What gave it away?" She forced a light tone. "The doll collection or the butterfly wallpaper?"

"The baseball bat and gloves, actually." Paul flashed Joy a grin that had her heart perform a somersault in her chest. "You were a tomboy, weren't you, Miss Cooper?"

"Pretty much, yes."

"And what are you now, when you're not being some stranger's Good Samaritan?"

"A schoolteacher."

"A schoolteacher." His brows arched and his lips pursed in a soundless whistle. "All prim and proper?"

He knew better, Paul thought, recalling with a stab the passion they had, all too briefly and incompletely, shared.

"Not really." Joy laughed, a bit self-consciously, thinking how different this Paul Mallik seemed to be from the man who had been her charge. Different, yet at the same time so familiar that she had to forcibly remind herself to keep her distance.

"Look," she said, twisting her fingers and slowly backing away from the bed toward the door, "Ma has dinner on the table. You're welcome to come down, if you're up to it."

Paul watched Joy's withdrawal with a sharp pang of regret. She had come to mean all manner of things to him. For these past days, she had been the sole center and the focus of his existence.

"I will miss you."

Joy froze, her heart suddenly lodged in her throat. "You're leaving." It wasn't a question.

"Yes."

"But couldn't you...?" Joy floundered. She had known it would come to this, of course. Heck, she hadn't wanted him in her hair in the first place. But... "What's your hurry? You've been sick."

"The ship's doctor will check me over. It is my duty to report back immediately, to let them know I'm alive and..."

"Couldn't you just phone them?" Reading the answer to that in his somber expression, Joy wondered miserably why she was doing this. She'd known it would only be a matter of time before Paul's memory came back. No one, except maybe Paul, could have wished for that harder than she. And she had known that, once he was himself again, sooner or later he would leave.

Yes, but did it have to be sooner?

"Given your brother Ernest's sentiments and the disruption of your festivities that I've already caused," Paul said, "I think it's best if I'm gone from here without fanfare. Unless you need me to come downstairs with you and explain? About our, uh, supposed marriage and so forth."

"No." Joy, swallowing, shook her head. "I can handle it."

Paul had no doubt she could. That and a lot more. Joy Cooper was quite a woman, a woman who had a great deal to offer a man.

But Paul suspected she didn't know it. Nor would she believe it if he pointed it out.

Getting up off the bed, he tugged on the slightly rumpled jacket of his borrowed suit. And then he looked at her for several long moments.

Joy quivered beneath the intensity of that look.

"Have I thanked you?" he asked, his voice vibrant with feeling. "For being there, for saving my life, as well as for everything else?"

"Don't." Tears threatened. Joy bit her lip to stem them. "I was happy to do it."

"Will you convey my thanks and apologies to your mother?"

"Sure." He's leaving.

"I will have the suit cleaned and sent back here in a few days."

"That'll be fine." Don't go. She *had* to say something. "Paul?"

"Yes, *carsya?*"

"If you could, I mean if there were some way that you could, you know . . . stay—"

"No." Paul stepped close and pressed a hard kiss onto her lips. "Thank you, sweet Joy. I'll never forget you for all you have done."

Joy caught up with him out on the promenade, some half a mile from her mother's house. It had taken no great detective work to figure out that this was the way he had gone—it was the only way back to the center of town.

On this unseasonably mild and sunny day, the Seacrest promenade was crowded with afternoon strollers, in-line skaters and people walking their dogs.

But Paul was not walking. He was sitting on a bench, half-hidden behind a stand of gnarled pine trees, with his elbows on his knees and his chin in his hands, staring out to sea with a faraway look on his face.

Joy almost ran by without seeing him, but something—perhaps a special kind of antenna she possessed where he was concerned—had drawn her gaze to the bench.

She plopped herself down beside him and also looked out to sea. "What're you thinking?"

Paul slowly turned his head, without lifting his chin from his hands. He didn't seem surprised to see her.

"Many things," he said. And, once she had acknowledged him with a glance of her own, turned his face back to the sea.

"Name one," Joy said,

"All right. What are you doing here?"

"Rescuing you again," Joy said. "But we'll get to that in a minute. First I want to know if you're married."

That brought his head around with a snap, but Joy kept her gaze firmly front and center. She knew she was on thin ice here and knew she couldn't pull off her plan if she looked at him and saw...well, discouraging things.

"So are you?" she persisted.

His reply was a long time coming. But when it came, his curt "No" made Joy's heart lift in song.

"Do you like it on that ship?" she asked.

"Joy." Paul's tone held a note of warning.

Joy waved him off. "Please, Paul, humor me. It's important. So do you?"

"Joy, where is this leading?" His eyes bored into her profile. "What're you up to?"

"Dammit, can't you just answer my question?" Joy swiveled to face him. "Jeez, but you're difficult to help."

"Help?" Paul sat up straight. "I don't need your help any longer. I'm fine now."

"No, you're not." She paused a beat. "So how do you like the navy?"

"I'm not in the navy."

"Well, the U.N., then—whatever."

With a resigned shake of his head—he did know Joy's single-mindedness by now, after all—Paul answered. "My term is nearly over, but, yes, I liked it well enough. In any case, it served its purpose."

"Which was?"

"To travel and see the world. Isn't that how the slogan goes?" Exasperation got the best of him. "Look, Joy, all I wanted was a few quiet moments to enjoy the American sun and fresh air before I go back to my ship."

"*Aha!*" Triumphantly, Joy shot to her feet. "Then you *do* like it here!"

"Well, of course, but—" Paul stared at Joy. A feeling of unease raised the hairs at the back of his neck. "You're crazy."

"Am I?" Joy, grinning, slowly shook her head. "You won't think so when you hear my proposition."

"Proposition?"

"Yes." Bending, she brought her face so close to his, Paul could have kissed her lips without moving.

"Stay here," she whispered. "With me."

"You're crazy," Paul said again, but without heat. His eyes were on the lips that were so tantalizingly close. He was crazy, too, he thought, for wanting to kiss her. And because, for just an instant, what she offered held the sweetest kind of promise.

Lunacy. Paul surged to his feet. "Impossible."

He turned his back on her.

Joy stepped around in front of him. "No it isn't. I read all about it in *Newsworld* just last week. Foreigners are marrying American citizens—"

That's as far as she got before Paul exploded. "So that's it!"

He didn't know when he'd been so angry. Or felt so betrayed. Yes, he did—earlier today, when Joy told him they were not really married. That she had used him.

And she wanted to use him again.

"This isn't about me, it's about you," he charged. "You're still trying to stick it to your faithless lover and parade me around as your stand-in husband! Well, count me out!"

Roughly, he shoved her aside and strode up the promenade with long, angry strides.

For several moments, Joy stared after him in motionless shock. Dammit, it wasn't just for her! It was for him, too. They both stood to gain if they married. Why wouldn't he see that?

Because she hadn't presented her case properly, that's why.

"Paul! Wait!" It wasn't in her to give up without a fight. Not when this could be so important for him. For them both. She ran after him, oblivious to walkers, bikers, dogs and kids. Oblivious to anyone but Paul, walking out of her life.

"Hear me out, darn you!"

Paul stopped finally and waited for her to catch up with him. Out of breath, panting, Joy stood in front of him and suddenly didn't know what to say. There was such pain in his eyes.

They studied each other for long, pulsing moments. Paul's somber expression mirrored precisely what Joy was suddenly feeling—a terrible sense of hopelessness and loss.

The world faded into the background. The shriek of the gulls, the laughter of children, the crash of the surf grew muted while the beat of Joy's heart seemed to grow louder and louder.

"It's the strangest thing," Paul finally said, very quietly.

"What is?" Joy asked when he said no more, only kept looking at her, searchingly, an expression of an amazed sort of wonder easing, but not erasing, the shadows of pain.

"That in such a short time I should have come to think of you as my dear friend. I've never been known to make friends quickly."

He gave her a brief, humorless smile and turned his face to the sea. "When I first woke up at your cottage, if I'd had even an inkling then of the sort of woman you are..."

"You would have run, screaming, back into the sea."

"No." Paul's smile grew wistful. "Tell me, Joy. Have you ever wanted something so much, you would have killed to have it?

"Of course not," he answered himself, not giving Joy a chance to reply. "You're Joy Marie Cooper, *American*. With all the rights and privileges and opportunities that entails. You've never known war, injustice or hunger, except in the abstract. You've never had to fight for anything, except perhaps a raise in your allowance."

"Now, just a darn minute." Much as she liked him and wanted him to stay, Paul's charges were lighting Joy's fuse. He made her sound so complacent, so stupidly fat and happy.

"I'll have you know, there's plenty I've fought for, many things I care about—the homeless, children, illiteracy—"

"Abstracts."

Ignoring the scoff, Joy kept right on talking. "—the environment, animal rights. There's plenty I care about and would fight for, so don't you dare accuse me—"

"And I never did." The last thing Paul wanted at this late juncture was a fight. She had done so much for him.

"You misconstrued what I said," he said. "Believe me, I *know* you care. Who'd know better? Without you, I—"

He shook his head, his tone urgent. "But, Joy, don't you see? I *envy* you. Most of the world envies you. Who you are, what you have. It's what I—we—want, too.

"To be free enough, full enough, educated enough to be able to care, to *do*. To have the chance to make a difference—"

Abruptly, Paul turned and stalked away.

Joy hop-skipped into step beside him.

He shoved his hands into his jacket pockets. "I applied for immigration many years ago," he said. "Straight out of university."

"And?" Joy's expressive eyes were asking him the same question he had asked himself as well as the American consulate time and time again: Why not him, when so may less qualified and deserving seemed to be welcomed with open arms?

He gave her the same answer he had been given. "Quotas." He spat the word.

Joy looked bewildered. Paul didn't blame her. He'd had it explained to him by experts and still it made no sense.

"I'm neither rich nor a refugee," he said. "My country, Gorska, has no special status in the political scheme of things. Gorska is sort of the Switzerland of Central America," he added in a feeble attempt at humor that made neither of them laugh. "Except poorer."

"But not poor enough. Is that it?" Joy wondered if she would ever understand the bureaucratic process. "What was your major?"

"Major?"

"At university," Joy elaborated when she noticed Paul's bewilderment. "Your field of study."

"Ah." The small sound was accompanied by a rueful half grin that made Joy want to hug him. "My mother and I never had occasion to discuss the terminology of higher education. She died when I was thirteen years old."

"I'm sorry."

Paul nodded. "Me, too." He paused a beat, then said, "In any case, my, uh, major was—is—marine biology."

"But the United Nations..." There were so many complexities here. Joy frowned in confusion. "How...?"

"They offered the best opportunities for pursuing the kind of research in which I am interested for my doctoral thesis. The migratory habits of large sea mammals—whales and so on—have always fascinated me."

"Then you did earn your master's degree." Joy's interjection was part question, part statement.

"Yes."

"But that's great!" Joy exclaimed. "The government is forever granting visas to people who want to pursue advanced degrees. And if you and I were married—"

"No." Paul stopped walking, grabbing her by the arm to stop her, as well. He spun her around to face him. "We are not going to be married, Joy."

"But why not? It only makes sense...."

"No. I will not enter into another deception. My God, Joy, have you already forgotten the trouble your last scheme caused?"

Joy waved that away with an impatient flick of the wrist. She stepped aside to let a group of cyclists pass. "I told you I can handle my family."

"Well, I can't."

"You'll get to stay in this country. You said you wanted that."

"Not this way." They faced each other like combatants in the middle of the Seacrest promenade. Passersby gave them curious glances. Neither Joy nor Paul noticed. "Not by *marrying you*," Paul said with finality. "No, sir. Never."

Joy was stung, but not about to show it, by his adamant refusal of her proposal of marriage. It was a darn good idea all around even if, as Paul had so quickly pointed out, it wasn't quite as selfless a plan as she would have liked to present it to be. So what? They would each get out of it what they wanted. Vindication for herself, education and a green card for Paul.

"I saved your life," she reminded him stiffly.

"And now I'm saving yours."

Paul decided he was through arguing. He had spotted a police cruiser parked on the street not twenty feet away. He intended to go to the officer sitting behind the wheel and ask for a lift to his ship in Astoria harbor before Joy and her so-called good intentions got completely out of hand.

"Listen to me." He caught her the shoulders. His eyes burned into hers. "I know what it's like to be in a marriage without love. It is hell. It is misery. Never will I enter into such a thing again."

"Not even for just a little while? For me?"

"Not for any length of time and especially not for you." He gave her a little shake. "You deserve better than that, *carsya mu*. Even if you don't know it."

"But—" With all that was at stake, this close to Paul, and with the moist warmth of his breath fanning her face, all Joy could think of were the kisses they had shared. Her mouth went dry and the objection she wanted to make fled from her mind.

"Don't look at me like that." Paul gave her another little shake.

Joy blinked in confusion. "Like what?"

"Like you want to make love with me."

"What?" Because it was true, and because he so obviously *didn't* want to make love with her, Joy wrenched herself free.

"Don't flatter yourself, Mr. Mallik. My, uh, proposition was strictly altruistic."

"Sure it was. And the sun never sets in Camelot." Paul turned away in annoyance. How dare she pretend she didn't have her own ax to grind with this ludicrous marriage proposal of hers?

Grimly he tugged at the cuffs of his shirt. But the sleeves were too short and all the tugging in the world wasn't going to make them protrude beyond the sleeve of the jacket. "I hope you won't think me ungrateful—"

"I will. I do already."

Their gazes clashed. Paul wouldn't release Joy's when she tried to tear hers away.

"I can never repay you for what you did," he said quietly. "You saved my life. And you've given me a couple of truly unforgettable days. I won't thank you for that by letting you commit another ill-conceived prank."

"Prank!"

"Shh." He pressed the tips of his fingers against Joy's lips to silence her, then replaced him with his mouth in a quick, hard kiss. "Goodbye, Joy Cooper. Have a good life."

Stunned, Joy watched him stride up to a Seacrest patrol car—Mike Jessup was the cop at the wheel. He was Ernie's best friend. She saw Paul bend to talk to Mike, then step back to let Mike get out of the car. Mike opened the back door of the cruiser, motioning with his hand for Paul to get in.

Before complying, Paul glanced back at Joy.

The wistfulness of his smile cut at Joy's heart.

Lifting his hand in a gesture of farewell, Paul swiveled, and slid into the seat.

Dammit. Tears stung Joy's eyes. She wasn't going to let him do this! To her or to himself!

Mike had just closed the door when Joy cried, "Paul! No! Wait . . . !"

Officer Jessup glanced up, startled, then muttered a disgruntled "What the hell?" as Joy barreled into him and bodily shoved him aside.

"Paul!" she cried, wrenching open the patrol car's back door and launching herself at the man inside. "Oh, Paul! Don't leave me!"

Mike's jaw dropped to his chest as, stunned, he watched his daughter's teacher, his best friend's sister, his brother-in-law Vernon's ex-fiancé, commence to kiss the breath out of the foreigner who had just requested to be taken to the *Explorer II* in Astoria. The man looked dazed and in shock when Joy finally let him come up for air.

"Paul, please don't leave me," she said brokenly, huge tears rolling down her cheeks as she cast a pitiful glance up at the bewildered trooper.

"Don't let him do this, Mike," she begged. "If not for me..."

Joy let the sentence hang on a shuddering breath. She cast a shy glance at Paul who was staring at her as if she'd sprouted horns or a second head.

And Paul could only gasp, speechless and horrified, when with a sad little hiccup—and an audacious wink that was meant just for him—Joy delivered the coup de grace.

"...then for the ba-by...."

*Chapter Seven*

"**W**hat!"

Paul and Mike ejaculated the word at the same time
and with similar expressions of shock. Until as recently
as yesterday—the day of Vern Harris's wedding to Sheila
MacKenzie—Mike had been under the impression that
Joy Marie Cooper had been left high, dry and shattered
by that tomcatting brother-in-law of his. So what in
blazes was this baby thing all about?

He drew himself up to his full professional height as
the stranger who'd asked to be driven to Astoria shot out
of the patrol car as if fired from a cannon, unceremoni-
ously dumping Joy Marie off his lap in the process.

"Just what in the hell's goin' on here, Joy Marie?"
Mike demanded to know in a voice that had folks on the
sidewalk slanting them inquisitive looks.

Joy, who had picked herself up and was huddled
against the police cruiser's chassis, snuffled into a tis-

sue. "You heard me, Mike. So could you please just drive us back to my ma's house?"

"Officer," Paul exploded, "I demand that you take me to my ship."

"Hold it!" *Demand* was not a word Mike enjoyed from folks in his custody, even if they had voluntarily put themselves there. "Just a blinkin' minute here, both o' you." He fixed Paul and Marie with a sternly official glare. "Nobody's going anywhere until I know what in blazes is going down. Now. Joy Marie."

"Yes?" Joy daintily dabbed at the corners of her eyes, darting a quick glance at Paul.

He was watching her, stone-faced, but inwardly seething. He had learned by now that Joy could be single-minded when there was something she set herself to do. But this was going too far.

"Did I hear you say something about a...a..." Mike faltered, flushed and noisily cleared his throat.

"Yes, Mike," Joy whispered, with a shy glance at Paul who was visibly fuming now. "I'm afraid you did."

"Are you saying that you and this man...?"

Joy wouldn't meet Mike's gaze. Her nod and mumbled "Uh-huh" were directed at her feet. And so she didn't see Paul toss up his hands with a muttered imprecation; she only felt herself suddenly gripped by the arm and bodily hauled a few steps aside.

"Just a moment, Officer," Paul said sharply to Mike who was preparing the take action to stop him. "Please," he added more quietly.

Turning his back on the officer, Paul stuck his face into Joy's. She was grimacing from the pain he was inflicting with his iron grip on her arm, but in his present state of mind, Paul was not about to ease up. On the contrary, he would dearly have loved to wring the woman's neck.

"Just what do you think you're doing?" he snarled through teeth that were clenched with fury. He kept thinking that this couldn't be happening to him. He had made his position clear to Joy. Why couldn't she accept it? Were all women schemers at heart?

"I'm saving you from making a terrible mistake," Joy hissed back. Defiance and stubbornness were carved in every line of her face and blazed in the eyes that unflinchingly met Paul's. "I said I'd marry you so you can stay in this country and, by damn, marry you I will."

"You're crazy," Paul said flatly after a long exchange of mutually fulminating glares.

"No, you are," Joy countered, "if you persist in fighting me on this."

"Tell me, Miss Cooper," Paul said, after glancing away with a few viciously uttered choice Gorskan phrases. "This baby thing. Can you be honest enough to tell me what it's all about?"

"I *have* told you—"

Paul cut her short with a curt "*Funato!* Stop insulting my intelligence. You are pregnant by some other man, is that it?"

"No!" Joy was appalled that he would think her so completely underhanded, not to mention lacking in morals. She had her faults, she wanted her way, but she had always been well-meaning. "That's not it at all. I truly do want to help you...."

His silent regard warned her not to push it.

"All right, all right." Joy tossed up her hands in capitulation. "So I'll confess— I— Hell's bells!"

Glancing across Paul's shoulder, Joy saw her brother Ernie charging up to Mike. She knew that if she didn't act quickly, there would be trouble.

"Ernie's here," she told Paul in an agitated whisper. "So just play along, okay? I'm doing this for both of us."

And with that she threw her arms around Paul's neck.

"Kiss me," she hissed, her lips a mere fraction of an inch from his. Out of the corner of her eye she saw Ernie approaching.

"Please. Now," she whispered with such a melting come-hither glance, Paul would have had to be made from stone to resist it. He wasn't and didn't. Especially since the kisses Joy had plied him with earlier in the police car were still vividly hot on his lips.

Besides, the sinuous pressure of her body against his was more than any man could have resisted. Paul had had a taste of Joy before and didn't even try. His arms closed around her and his lips took possession with an urgency and heat that exploded out of him from a combination of anger and pure masculine need.

He was a man who, at thirty-three, was in the prime of his virility. She was a woman who, it seemed to him, was built for love—the quintessential Eve. The fact that she didn't seem to know this—something he sensed in the inherently innocent ardor of her kisses—made her all the more desirable to him.

But desirable enough to marry? *Donde!* No!

He wrenched his mouth from the sweet seduction of hers just as a male voice at his back growled, "Like I told you earlier, Mallik, I'd like to have a word with you."

Big brother Ernie.

Paul closed his eyes on an inward groan and took a deep breath. Reaching up, he tried to remove Joy's hands from around his neck, but she wouldn't cooperate. He glared at her and their gazes dueled a moment before she shifted hers past him to Ernie.

"Butt out, Ern," she said, "This is strictly between Paul and me."

"Like hell." Ernie clamped a viselike hand on Paul's shoulder, spun him around and, with one well-placed punch, sent him sprawling. "That's for trying to walk out on my sister."

Down on the ground, Paul slowly raised up on one elbow, rubbing and flexing his jaw. Considering his options, he looked from Ernie's glowering face into that of the policeman and on into Joy's visage of ashen distress.

He gave some thought to getting up and walloping Ernest Cooper—no idle dream given the fact that he was a trained master of hand-to-hand combat. Or he could get up, demand once more to be taken to his ship and let the devious Miss Cooper stew in her own juices.

*I saved your life.*

Though he hardly needed a reminder, the words popped into his mind. And it was true—she had.

She was pregnant.

Could it be that now she needed for him to save *her* life? Or, at least, her pride and reputation? Hmm...

As he lay on the ground, taking a couple of seconds to consider his choices, Paul kept his gaze firmly fixed on Joy's. The mixture of wretchedness and empathy he saw there, the regret for her brother's punch, made up his mind.

"I guess," he said slowly, "I know when I'm licked."

Something flashed in Joy's eyes then, and it wasn't the relieved gladness he might have expected to see. It was an expression much more like pain, or intensified gret, with a good dose of shame thrown in to further confuse him.

"Oh, Paul," she said, in a small voice. She took a hesitant step toward him. "I—"

But something of the emotions that still churned in him—remnants of anger, confusion and a lingering sense of betrayal—must have crept past the rigid mask of his face. She didn't come closer, only looked at him in misery as she quietly said, "I'm sorry."

A week later they were married.

Paul had spent most of that time, along with the rest of the *Explorer II*'s crew, at the Salt Flats Motel in Astoria, while the ship was in dry dock, being repaired from the storm damage. He had moved his belongings—a footlocker and a couple of duffel bags—off the ship. It felt good to be wearing his own clothes again and even better to know he would soon be permanently out of uniform.

Since his U.N. tenure had been coming up for renewal anyway, there had been no problem with mustering out a few weeks early. His passport was in order, and an exchange of faxes with the nearest Gorskan consulate, in San Francisco, had supplied everything the American Immigration and Naturalization Service needed to know about Pavel Eduardo Mallik. His academic records, his honorable discharge from the Gorskan navy and the fact that he had never been in jail were all duly noted.

He was fingerprinted and certified to be in perfect health after the most thorough physical he had ever undergone.

He had seen Joy, his blushing bride-to-be, off and on, but alone only once.

She had come to him at the motel. She had called to say that she needed some of his documents for legalities to do with the upcoming wedding, but that she'd like a chance to talk to him, as well. Alone.

There had been no chance for them to speak privately after that Easter Sunday fiasco in Seacrest had drawn to a close. Ernie had hustled Joy off to her mother's and Paul, with Joy's unexpected support, had, as originally requested, been driven to Astoria by Mike the policeman.

After Joy's arrival at the motel, at her request, they had gone into the coffee shop. The waitress had poured them each a cup of coffee. Neither had spoken for a while. It was two in the afternoon. Except for a couple of businessmen at the counter, the place was deserted. Nobody paid any attention to them as they sat at their window table and studied each other in silence.

Paul noted things about Joy he hadn't really noticed before. The color of her eyes, for instance. Blue, yes, but not blue like his, a single cerulean shade. Her blue was changeable, as changeable as her moods—now sparkling like a sun-kissed lake, now almost black like a gathering thundercloud.

And then, he remembered with a quickening in his blood, there was the brilliantly sapphire shade of blue her eyes assumed when they kissed.

She had freckles. They dotted the bridge of her nose and the top of her cheeks like flecks of cinnamon streusel on his mother's sugar cake. One could almost imagine the feel and taste of licking them off....

Her lips were full and, in repose, rested against each other in a determined and stubborn line that bespoke her strong will. Yet they curved sweetly upward at the corners, thus preventing the appearance of mulishness.

As he watched and studied her, being obliquely watched and studied in return, Joy absently sucked the side of her lower lip between her teeth. Paul's breath hitched; he found her small action immensely arousing.

ANNE PETERS                                    109

Probably, he told himself wryly, because he'd been spending his nights reliving and tasting her kisses and, as a consequence, had been walking around in a half-aroused state while awake ever since.

Apropos of... Perhaps he should ask what, if any, plans Joy had made with regard to the...intimate side of their marriage.

His jeans suddenly felt uncomfortable and he shifted in his chair. He cleared his throat rather noisily and, frowning, tore his gaze away from Joy's mouth. He looked around, needing some other focus, something to do, and his eyes lit on the sugar container. He hauled it across the table and dumped some sugar into his coffee.

"So," he said, sounding gruff even to himself as he vigorously stirred. "You wanted to see me?"

He lifted the cup to his mouth, took a healthy swallow and almost gagged. *"Donde,"* he spluttered, barely keeping himself from spitting the brew back out.

"What happened?" Joy was all concern. "Did you burn yourself?"

With a grimace, Paul swallowed, shaking his head. "No. But I *detest* sweet coffee. Yuck."

Joy frowned. "Then why did you put all that sugar in?"

Paul let the look he sent her speak for itself.

"Ah." Comprehending, a small snort of laughter escaped her before she could bite down on her lower lip and stifle it. "I'm sorry."

"You already said that last Sunday."

Paul's reply instantly sobered Joy Marie.

Watching the light fade from her eyes before she could hide them by lowering her eyelids, Paul wished he had kept his mouth shut.

"That's one of the main things I came to talk to you about," Joy said, staring into her coffee. "I want you to know I, uh, I told my family the truth."

"About what?" Paul couldn't keep himself from asking a little bitterly. Part of him deeply resented the position Joy had put him in even as another part of him realized—and appreciated—that by her actions he'd been handed a rare chance at fulfilling a dream.

He was willing to help her out, more than willing to settle the debt of gratitude he owed her, but he didn't much like being manipulated. All she would have had to do was explain the situation and ask for his help.

He toyed with his cup of unwanted coffee. "About us?"

"About everything," Joy said, raising her head and looking him full in the face. "Everything."

"The baby?"

"There is no baby."

"What!"

"I made it up."

"You . . ." Paul was aghast. "For God's sake, why?"

"To make you stay."

For a long time neither of them spoke. Their gazes clung.

"Why is that so important to you?" Paul finally asked.

"I don't know." Joy looked down at the spoon with which her fingers had been nervously toying. "All that stuff about the contributions you'd be able to make . . . And, too, you're so darn qualified . . . I got to thinking it just wasn't fair, a person like you not being able to come here and live a good life. I wanted to help you."

"Even when I no longer wanted your help?"

"Yes."

"Because you knew what was best for me?"

"Yes, dammit." Sparks shot from her eyes, but then, with an abashed smile, Joy slumped. "I don't like to give up when I think I have a good idea."

"So I've come to learn." With a grin, Paul shook his head. "And here I thought that I was the one helping you."

In response to Joy's expression of puzzled inquiry, he elucidated. "By legitimizing another man's baby."

"Oh, Paul." Tears rushed into Joy's eyes. "You were willing to do that? For me?"

"Am I not doing it?"

"Oh, Paul," Joy said again, shyly touching Paul's arm, draped along the tables' edge. "Thank you."

"You're welcome." Paul started to cover Joy's hand with his own, but she drew hers away and looked down again into her coffee.

"I told my family the whole thing," she said. "About finding you on the beach, the amnesia thing. Everything. And so I came here to say that there, uh, there really doesn't have to be a wedding if...if you really don't..." She glanced up with a helpless shrug. "You know."

"If I really don't want to," Paul finished for her. He looked down at his hands, not sure how he felt. "What prompted you to—what's that expression?—spill the beans?"

"Yes, that's it."

In response to his other question, Joy shrugged again. "I don't know. I don't like lying to Ma, and I've never been very good at charades. Besides which, I knew that it was a lousy stunt I pulled. That, uh, baby thing."

Paul inclined his head, mutely conceding that, yes, it had indeed been a lousy stunt. He toyed with his cup. Joy toyed with hers. Neither spoke for a moment.

"I came to tell you I'm willing to call off the marriage," Joy finally said. "If you want me to," she hastened to add, lest Paul think she was trying to renege on him.

"And if I don't?"

Joy's gaze flew to his with a startled expression, telling Paul this was not the reply she had expected. "Are you saying you don't?"

"I'm not saying anything. I'm asking you a question, weighing my options, if you will. Before, thanks to your rather public shenanigans, I had no options or, at least, none that were viable to me. But now..."

He gestured with his hand. "Enlighten me. What will you do if I don't want to call off the wedding?"

"Well, I—" Discomfited by the unidentifiable gleam in Paul's eyes, Joy fidgeted, hemmed and then burst out, "I just thought that's what you wanted. To call it off. I mean, what about those other things you said? About loveless marriages?"

"I meant every word."

"And about dreams? That they shouldn't be built on deception and... and... Well, what about that?"

"I meant every word of that, too."

Joy stared at him helplessly. "Then I don't understand...."

"Don't you? It's quite simple really." Paul placed his elbows and forearms on the table and leaned forward. "Part of the reason you coerced me into accepting your—albeit unusual—proposal of marriage was because you thought it would help me. Correct?"

A little hesitantly because she didn't know where he was going with this, Joy nodded.

"All right." He raised his fingertips off the table and let them drop again. "Likewise, the only reason I accepted was because I wanted to help *you*."

"Ye-es?" Joy drew the word into two syllables.

"Do the reasons you gave for wanting to pass me off as your husband still exist?"

"You mean . . . ?"

"The town gossip and your Bernard Ferris, yes."

"Well, of course." Joy ducked her head and giggled. "And the name is Vernon Harris, not Bernard—"

"Whatever." Paul gestured impatiently. "Don't you still want to show him that 'Joy Marie Cooper went and found herself another man, a better man,' I believe your words were?"

Joy flushed at the memory of that scene with her mother that Paul had overheard.

"Sure, but . . ." She glanced up at Paul helplessly.

"No buts," he said. "I owe you my life."

He paused. And then he said, "Besides," and his eyes began to smolder. "I think you and I will do very well together. In bed."

Joy flushed hotly. She didn't know where to look, she was so embarrassed by the turn of their conversation. No man had ever spoken to her in this way. So directly. About things . . . sexual. There had really only ever been Vernon for her, and he . . . well, he certainly hadn't . . . out loud . . .

Nor had he ever made her feel like this—all hot and confused and . . . and *wanting*. "B-but—"

Joy closed her mouth and compressed her lips, vexed with herself. She was stuttering, for crying out loud. And Paul was probably laughing at her, shocking her on purpose.

She slanted him a glare. He wasn't laughing. Quite the contrary. His eyes smoldered and his face was all somber intensity.

Oh, God. Joy's heart stood still and her thoughts turned to mush. Just so Paul would look at her the moment before he...

She swallowed convulsively. "Paul," she whispered. "Please..."

"Please what, *carsya?*"

His voice was low, and huskier than Joy had ever heard it. The foreign word he uttered brushed soft as velvet against the drum of her ear. The way he spoke made her realize that she wasn't the only one feeling things here.

The knowledge went a long way toward restoring her poise. "Please don't look at me like that," she entreated. "And don't speak to me...like that."

"I speak only the truth."

"Yes, well...maybe to you that's all it is. But I—that is, we here in America...well, you see we don't—"

"You don't!"

He said it so comically, Joy had to laugh. She shook her head, chagrined. "You're impossible."

"And you are very charming," Paul said seriously. He stood up. "I'll be right back with those documents you wanted."

The wedding ceremony had been a quiet affair. Paul had supplied the ring. His mother's. He had carried it everywhere as his talisman. Had never parted with it, had not even given it to Anna. Yet it seemed right to him that Joy wear it and he hadn't questioned the feeling.

Ernie had been the best man, an irony that wasn't lost on either of the men. But there wasn't anyone else—Paul had been friendly with most of the *Explorer*'s multinational officers, but close friends with none. At least not so close he would have wanted them at his wedding. Or, more to the point, at a wedding that was only a sham.

Everyone in attendance knew it for what it was, as well. And as a result, the mood was subdued. In the course of the brief civil ceremony, many uneasy glances were exchanged by Joy's family. The procedure clearly didn't sit well with any of them, but the underlying message seemed to be, *Well, if this is what Joy wants...*

Joy was Marie Cooper's youngest child, the girl Ernest, Sr.—so Marie had told Paul, almost apologetically, earlier that day—had so desperately wanted. They had named her Joy because theirs had been so great. She'd been a golden little girl and the boys had adored her. Protected her, especially after their father's death. And they'd indulged her. Always.

"It's a wonder she turned out as well as she did," Marie had said to Paul. "Her heart is good, the best. She cares about things."

Paul knew this, of course.

"Even as a child she was always toting home every hurt little critter, right down to the dead little starfish she'd find on the beach. And the boys would go find her a live one and exchange it, and then make like she'd cured the dead one she'd dragged home. We could none of us ever stand to see her disappointed or hurt.

"Vernon did hurt her, though. Badly. Her pride, I suspect, more than anything, but nevertheless. She took it hard, his tomcatting around with that Sheila MacKenzie. That girl never was any better than she needed to be, but that's neither here nor there.

"Vern dumped Joy two days before the wedding—this was a month ago, just before spring break. We had planned a big affair with all the hoopla and trimmings that make the day special. People were coming from out of town. Some had already arrived. Gifts, everything. It was terrible. Joy was so heartbroken, she was sick. Everybody here in town felt sorry for her. I think she found that the hardest to bear. She took sick leave and up and left for Seattle. And then you happened. At the cottage. It brought her back to life and I thank you for that.

"She's willful, Paul. And she's spoiled. But never think she's bad," Marie had pleaded with a look of entreaty. "Please don't."

*Never think she's bad.*

Paul was to remind himself of Marie's words that evening when he and Joy were back in Astoria, alone at last.

They had not previously discussed living arrangements. In fact, Paul had not thought to check out of his motel. His clothes and belongings were still there. Since he didn't own a suit and was technically still a part of the *Explorer II*'s crew, he had worn his officer's uniform for the wedding.

Now, after trailing Joy up the stairs to the door of her apartment, he was thinking that there would be time enough to collect his things and properly move in with Joy in the morning.

Joy had been very quiet and subdued the entire day. Her responses to the justice of the peace had been mumbled, and she had turned her head when the time had come for Paul to kiss the bride. His lips had merely grazed her cheek. She had spoken only when spoken to during the very nice postwedding supper that Marjorie and Jolene had prepared, and to Paul not at all.

Paul had told himself that she was suffering a delayed reaction to everything that had led up to their nuptials, and he had left her alone.

For himself, once having arrived at this juncture, he had made up his mind to give the arrangement his best shot. People married for all manner of reasons all over the world. In his country, arranged marriages were still quite often the thing, though not as much as, say, twenty or thirty years ago.

Love. Pshaw!

Paul knew from personal experience that the romantic kind that poets liked to go on about was a highly overrated commodity. In fact, he'd go so far as to say it was a disease.

He had been afflicted by that disease only once. And the cure for it had been so painful, he would do anything, go anywhere, to avoid catching the sickness again.

What had he said to Joy? That to live in a loveless marriage was hell? He'd been wrong to put it that way, because it wasn't the state of lovelessness that was hell, it was the state of *one-sided love* that was hell in marriage.

To love and not be loved back, that was the hell.

Because in a marriage like that, eventually even friendship would no longer be possible.

And so he had decided that in the marriage he had made with Joy Marie Cooper, they would be friends as well as—and he saw no reason to expect otherwise, given the heat of Joy's kisses—lovers. To give each other pleasure, in bed and out, this was good. A bonus for each of them.

Climbing the stairs to Joy's front door, Paul was very much looking forward to enjoying that bonus.

He stood quietly while Joy, visibly nervous, fumbled with the key.

"Shall I help you?" he asked.

"No, no." Joy's voice was little more than a breath whisper. "I can manage. There."

The key was in the lock and she turned to face him though her eyes shied away from making contact with his. "Thanks, Paul. I, uh, I'll be fine now. The motel only a—"

"The *motel?*" Paul didn't think he'd heard correctly. "You don't mean that you intend for me to...?"

"Why, yes," Joy said quickly. "Yes, of course."

"But..." This was so unexpected, Paul was reduced to splutter, "But we're married—"

"In name only."

"You mean you don't intend for us to...?"

"No. No, I don't." Though she tried to sound calm and determined, Joy's hand, turning the key, shook even more than it had before. "The motel is only about a block from here. You can see the sign from our front lawn."

Her door swung open and she stepped inside, turned and, with her eyes meeting his at last, said, "I'll be going back to work on Monday and I've got a lot of catching up to do beforehand since I took off that extra time. I'm not sure when I'll be able to see you next. Why'nt you give me a call if you need anything. Okay?"

It was beyond Paul to speak at that moment. He could only gaze at her in mute consternation. And by the time he'd gathered his wits enough to voice his objections, she had said a quiet "Good night" and closed the door.

*Never think she's bad.*

Staring at the closed door, Paul heard again those words of Marie's and a grim chuckle escaped him. So now what? he asked himself. Should he do as this unpredictable *bride* of his requested and seek out his lonely motel room bed?

What if the INS had informers posted outside? Having come this far, did he really want to jeopardize his chances to stay in the States?

*Donde.* No, he didn't!

Grimly, Paul considered pounding on Joy's door and demanding she let him in. But then, with a muttered oath, he decided to let it be.

Weary, he turned up his jacket collar, stuffed his hands in the pockets of his pants and made himself as comfortable as the cramped space of Joy's landing permitted.

# Chapter Eight

Joy had not slept well. In fact, not at all. She discovered that self-recriminations, second thoughts and unfaced longings made for very uncomfortable bedfellows.

About five in the morning, she gave up the struggle. She marched herself into the living room and there gave herself the dressing-down she so richly deserved.

"You idiot," was how she started. "You just *had* to try and be noble, didn't you? He was *willing* to stay the night. You *wanted* him to. So what in the *world* is your problem?"

*He didn't really want to stay. He just felt obligated because it was our wedding night.*

"So? Here would have been your chance to *make* him want to stay in the future. You could have loved him so hard...."

*I do not love him!*

"Did I say you did? I meant love in the physical sense. And don't try to tell *me* you don't want him that way."

*Boy, do I.*

"Well, you blew it, didn't you? Did you see his face?"

*Don't remind me.*

"He was crushed. I tell you he *wanted* to stay. And not because he figured he had to. So what're you planning to do, Joy Marie? Go to him?"

*God, no.*

"Why the heck not?"

*I just couldn't. My pride...*

"Well, girl, then I hope you and your pride'll live happily ever after."

Joy had herself a good cry after that, but there was no one around to say, "There, there."

Things got worse.

It was barely seven o'clock when a knock sounded on the apartment door. "Young lady!"

Mrs. Ross.

Joy put down her teacup with a sense of impending doom. The urge to pretend she wasn't home was strong, but quickly suppressed just the same. She went to the door and opened it. "Good morning, Mrs. Ross."

"Nothing good about it. There's a man sleeping on your doorstep."

With her steel-blue hair in rollers and her lumpy shape wrapped in faded chenille, old Edna would have been a sight for Joy to giggle over in happier times.

As it was, she could only stare past her at Paul.

He was scrambling stiffly to his feet, pointed his hands ceilingward in a mighty stretch, yawned and then politely said, "Good morning, *eposa*. And you, Mrs. Ross."

He bowed to the landlady, who was speechless for once.

Paul gestured from himself to Joy. "A little tiff, soon forgotten. Isn't that right, my love?" he added, addressing Joy.

"Uh . . ." Joy, too, was speechless.

"Excuse me, won't you?" Paul seized the moment to squeeze past Joy into the apartment.

Joy glanced helplessly after him, then back at Mrs. Ross. "A friend," she said lamely.

"Your *husband*," Edna corrected, with every one of her myriad wrinkles set in lines of the utmost disapproval.

"Joy Marie, I find I cannot tolerate any longer the kind of shenanigans we've had on your account this past week."

"But, Mrs. Ross—" Joy meant to tell her all would be quiet again from now on.

Edna wouldn't even let her speak. "I'm sorry, young lady, but you knew the rules when you moved in here. For one, no married couples—"

"But, Mrs. Ross—" Joy wanted to point out that no such rule had ever been stated. And besides . . .

But her landlady didn't even pause for breath. "—no callers after 9:00 p.m. and no intoxication. You, young lady, have broken every one of those rules. Epilepsy, indeed. I want you gone by the end of the month."

"But that's too soon," Joy protested.

"You've got a husband now. Put him to work." Edna turned to go. "Good day to you, Joy Marie."

Joy stared after her, one hand still raised in mute objection. Realizing the futility of it, she limply let it drop.

But then her temper flared. Darn the old bat anyway! With a succinct, but choice oath, Joy resoundingly slammed the apartment door shut.

And damn Paul Mallik for his part in this, too!

"Problems?" Rebuttoning the cuffs of his dress shirt, Paul strolled out of the bathroom. He had washed his face and hands and combed his hair. His uniform jacket was flung casually across one shoulder. In all, he looked disgustingly fit and well rested.

Joy, who felt like yesterday's newspaper left in the rain, was in no mood to share her troubles. "Nothing I can't handle, I assure you."

"Now why doesn't that surprise me?" Paul fastened the top button of his shirt and tightened his tie.

Joy watched him with a mixture of remorse, guilt and anger. Anger being the easiest to deal with, she demanded, "What were you doing on my doorstep?"

"Sleeping."

"Sleeping?"

"That's right." Paul shrugged into his jacket and, his motions clipped now with suppressed anger, tugged down the cuffs of his shirt.

"Whatever for?" Joy asked incredulously.

"Appearances." Fed up with her, Paul's tone grew sharp. "Remember the INS, *Mrs*. Mallik? Guess what? They expect us to share the same roof, at least part of the time. And *certainly* on our wedding night."

"Oh my gosh." Joy stared at him, aghast. How could she have forgotten about the INS? "Gee, Paul, I'm sorry. I—"

"What?" Paul drawled sarcastically. "Didn't think? What a departure, since we both know how coolheaded and careful you usually are. But, hey, it's done, so let's forget it, shall we? I, for one, am in dire need of a shower, a shave and some coffee. Not necessarily in that order."

He strode to the door. "Have a good day, Mrs. M."

* * *

It was only nine o'clock when Joy showed up at her mother's. Ernie was there, having coffee, as was his custom most days. It was his way of making sure his mother was well and didn't need anything. Marie was already dressed for church.

Both looked surprised to see Joy.

"You're out early for a new bride," her mother remarked with arched brows.

Joy didn't reply. She walked to the stove and helped herself to coffee. Marie and Ernie exchanged pointed glances.

"Where's the husband?" Ernie growled. "Don't tell me I gotta go haul his butt back from somewheres already."

Joy shot him a glare. "Very funny."

"So where is he?"

"I don't know." Joy avoided looking at either Ernie or Marie. "At the motel, I guess."

"You guess?" Marie sent her son another troubled glance. "Are you telling us you didn't—"

"We didn't sleep together, no." Joy turned to face them, telling herself she sure didn't know what they were acting so shocked for. She said, "I don't know why that should surprise you. You knew the kind of wedding it was."

"Yes, but the Immigration Service," Marie pointed out. "Have you considered . . . ?"

"Look, it's Paul's problem, too, all right?" Joy plunked down her mug, sloshing coffee. "I don't know why everybody's coming down on me, all of a sudden. First old lady Ross, and now . . ."

"Old lady Ross?" Ernie echoed. "What's she done?"

"Given me notice, that's what."

"Notice?" Joy's mother cried. "Whatever for?"

Miserable, Joy related the gist of her landlady's early morning visit. "I've got to be out by Tuesday."

"Why, that loony old bat," Ernie muttered. The Coopers might have their differences, but when the chips were down they stuck together. "What're you gonna do?"

"Move to the cottage, I thought."

"Yeah, that'll do. What about that chimney fire, though?"

"I was hoping you'd help get that taken care of."

"Consider it done," Ernie said. "Need help moving your stuff? Den and I can each bring our trucks...."

"Thanks, Ern." Tears filled Joy's eyes and she quickly turned and busied herself at the sink, dumping her untasted coffee and rinsing the mug.

"I didn't mean to snap at you guys," she said in a voice thick with swallowed tears. "It's just that I've made such a mess—"

In spite of her efforts, Joy's voice broke. "Oh, damn," she cried weakly. "I'm sorry. I really didn't want to do this."

"Hush." Her mother's arm came around her. "When things are this bad, they can only get better, right?"

To please her mother, Joy nodded. But inside she knew they wouldn't. That once again she'd messed up a relationship.

She didn't stay at her mother's much longer after that. And she declined Ernie's well-meant invitation to come spend the day with Jolene and the kids. She went home and packed some stuff and drove to the beach house.

She made several such trips to the cottage that day, mostly to bring over small household items that could be transported by car.

She studiously avoided the spare room that Paul had occupied. But even so, after making her last run, as she set about restoring at least superficial order in her bedroom, as well as the living room, Paul's presence was everywhere.

Out in the back porch hung his wet suit. It had dried stiff as a board. The saltwater, of course.

Joy took it off the peg, ran a finger over the stitching of his name and recalled how she had felt peeling his cold and all-but-lifeless body out of it. She had been full of worry, fear and panic.

Full of pretty much the same emotions she felt now, thinking of Paul. And thinking of him going out of her life.

It was so silly. Or so she told herself. She knew him less than two weeks. She couldn't have gotten used to having him around in such a short time.

But she had. More, she had married him. And as much as she might like it to be otherwise, she had come to care for him.

On the way home for the night, Joy took a detour via the Salt Flats Motel.

She was told Paul was out. Had been all day. Any message?

Joy shook her head. No. No message.

With plenty of time on his hands to think that Sunday, Paul had reached several conclusions. One, he needed to get out of the motel and into some digs of his own.

Two, even though he would not be able to apply for a regular job until the processing of his papers was concluded, he would nevertheless need something constructive to do or go out of his mind.

Three, whatever else he did, he would *not* approach Joy Marie Cooper—Mallik—again.

She talked of pride? Well, he, too, had his pride—male pride, personal pride, professional pride. Though he might be nothing more to Joy than a hapless charity case she had happened to fish from the sea, he was *somebody*. He was Gorskan and from a fine family. He was an officer and a gentleman.

Though far from rich, he was a man of some means—funds had already been transferred from his accounts in Gorska to an Astoria bank. And he was a scientist with a master's degree that he would turn into a Ph.D. at the earliest opportunity.

Oh, yes, he was somebody. Somebody who would have gladly shared who and what he was with the woman he had taken as his wife.

If Ernie Cooper was surprised to see his new brother-in-law drive up to the door of his stevedoring place in a brand-new, fully loaded Jeep Cherokee Monday morning, he gave no sign of it.

"Nice rig," he said.

"Thanks." Paul glanced at the gleaming truck with proprietary pride. "I bought it in Portland yesterday."

"Ah."

"They told me at the service station where to find you," Paul said, looking around with interest. "I don't know why, but somehow I'd gotten the idea you were a fisherman."

"I am. Among other things." Ernie signaled to one of the other men to take over and went out through the large double doors leading out to the dock, without inviting Paul to come along.

With a mental shrug, Paul followed anyway.

"You know anything about boats?" Ernie asked when they stood side by side on the dock, looking out over the water.

This time, Paul's shrug was a physical one. "I've been around a few."

Ernie slanted him a squinting glance. "I expect you have, at that." He pointed to one of the trawlers tied up at the dock. "See that one over there? That's the *Marie*, one of our dad's old boats. We still run her from time to time.

"Dennis has the *Joy Marie II* out right now," he went on. "She's the replacement of the boat that took our dad down to the bottom. They just left this morning and won't be back for a week or ten days. I mostly just go out for crab these days. There's too much to do around here. Friend of mine's got my boat out right now."

"Nice operation you've got here."

Ernie nodded, then sent Paul another squinting glance. "You lookin' for a job?"

"Thanks for asking—" It occurred to Paul that neither he nor his brother-in-law had ever called each other by name. Small wonder. He gave an inward chuckle. Theirs had not exactly been an amiable relationship so far. Yet, oddly, he liked the man. Quite a lot.

And perhaps odder still, given the circumstances, he felt quite sure that Ernie liked him, too.

"—Ernest." Paul made it a point to add Joy's brother's name to his thanks for the job offer, and the man's quick glance of surprise indicated that the point had been taken.

"Perhaps in a week or two, after the paperwork is completed, I might be." He looked Ernie in the eye. "Are you offering me one?"

Ernie shrugged, visibly discomfited. "Joy Marie told us you're a marine biologist. Not much call for one of those in my line of business."

"We both deal in fish," Paul pointed out reasonably. "I wouldn't mind helping out around here. At least until I..."

He hesitated because while standing here beside his brother-in-law, he'd gotten a sudden vision of how things might have been. If Joy had been as willing as he to make their arrangement into something more closely resembling a marriage. Disappointment was a bitter pill in his mouth that he had to swallow before he could complete the sentence without betraying his disillusionment.

"Until I get my bearings," he finished lamely, his surge of enthusiasm abruptly spent.

"I, uh, I was kind of surprised to see sis over at Ma's yesterday," Ernie said, frowning down at his boots. "Thought I'd see you with her—Paul." He glanced at Paul as he tagged on the name. "It being the first day of your marriage and all."

"Yes, well—" Not knowing what Joy might have told her family about the future of their arrangement, Paul wasn't at all sure what to say to Ernest. "I had some things to do and—"

"She says you won't be living together," said Ernie.

"Er, yes," Paul hastened to concur. "That's correct. Unless it becomes necessary."

"Paul," Ernie said. "I know it's probably none of my business, but—"

"Leave it, Ernie." Paul laid a hand on his brother-in-law's arm. "I don't know how much you know about Joy and me..."

"Enough," Ernie muttered.

"...but we've reached a kind of mutually advantageous understanding, I suppose you could call it."

Ernie snorted and spat into the bay.

Though Paul agreed with Ernie's assessment of the situation, he didn't let on. "Your sister saved my life. I owe her for that. Which brings me to the reason I came here. I want to repay her for what she did, but I have a feeling she wouldn't want me to."

"Prob'ly not." Ernie scowled into the distance.

"I don't remember much about the day she rescued me," Paul went on, "but I do remember—besides hearing you all talk about it—that chimney fire at the beach cabin. Ernie, I want to fix the damage to the place."

"Yeah?"

"But I don't want Joy to know I'm doing it."

"That so."

"In fact, I don't even want her to know where I am."

"Ahhh."

A gleam of understanding had come into Ernie's eye. And though Paul suspected that Ernie's understanding might be faulty—like, for instance, he might think Paul was hoping to accomplish a warming trend in his relationship with Joy by doing this work for her—if it meant he'd get Ernie's cooperation, he wasn't about to correct it.

Still, he thought it best to be forthright. "I really just want a chance to do something for your sister and, at the same time, have a quiet place to stay in which to sort things out for myself. I seem to recall that the cottage is fairly isolated."

"Sure is. Not a soul around for miles." Ernie considered Paul thoughtfully for a moment. "So, what you're saying is, you wanna move in there for while. Is that it?"

"And do the work," Paul hastened to stress. "But, yes. That's it."

"Without sis knowing about it. Is that right?"

Paul nodded, wondering at the grin that hovered at the corners of Ernest Cooper's mouth. "That's right, yes."

"Well, all right, then." Briskly, rubbing his hands, Ernie led the way back into the building and into a cramped and messy office. "I got the key to the place right here. Sis asked me to send some repairmen out about that chimney."

He grinned at Paul, the first time he'd ever done so. "I guess you're it."

"I'll need directions, too," Paul said.

"Well, sir, then you just pay close attention...."


Joy telephoned Paul Monday morning before work, too. She'd gotten to thinking about what he'd said about the INS and—

Who was she kidding? She missed Paul. Period. He had been the focus of her life since she had scooped his sodden carcass off the beach and she couldn't stand not knowing how and where he was.

Too, how could she impress anyone with her hunk of a husband, if he wasn't even around?

Somehow, her wedding jitters—she had *coerced* Paul into marriage, no matter how much he put a good face on it—had made her temporarily lose sight of their objectives.

She *had* to get a hold of Paul and get things back on track.

"Salt Flats Motel."

"Paul Mallik's room, please."

"Could you hold, please?"

Waiting, Joy shifted the phone to her other ear and held her breath to slow her thundering heart. What was the matter with her anyway? She was only going to talk—

"Miss?"

"Yes?"

"Mr. Mallik checked out."

"He did!" Joy's heart dropped into her shoes. "When, for heaven's sake? It's only a little after seven and he was still registered last night at eight."

"I'm sorry."

"No. I mean, wait." Joy closed her eyes and counted to ten. Calmer, she said, "Look, could you check his room, please? It's very important that I find him. Maybe he just paid you, but didn't really check out yet."

"He checked out, miss."

"But—"

"I saw him drive away just a minute ago. Sorry."

Clutching the phone, Joy nodded. She was sorry, too. About many things.

Joy had dreaded her first day back at work. Not the teaching part of it—her third graders adored her as much as she adored them. No, it was the time not spent teaching that she dreaded. The time in the staff room, the breaks and the socializing with her colleagues that she always used to look forward to.

Predictably, Rosa Mertz, the principal of the Roger Cameron School, took the lead in congratulating Joy on her marriage. Of course she, as well as the rest of the staff, had heard all about Joy's "pregnancy" through the town grapevine. But none of them knew the true facts, since only Joy's family had been privy to the corrected and accurate chain of events leading up to the precipitous Cooper-Mallik nuptials.

"It was all so sudden," Joy heard over and over again, and by lunchtime, the pointed glances at her midsection, in addition to her unceasing worry over Paul's whereabouts, made her want to scream.

In trying to explain the unexplainable—namely how a man so recently missing from a passing ship could have fallen in love, impregnated and married one of their own local teachers—Joy found herself having to lie more and more creatively.

"I don't even know what I said to whom anymore," she wailed to her mother when she rushed over there during her lunch hour. "How did I get myself into this, anyway?"

"I believe it's called acting on impulse," Marie said dryly. "You planning to eat lunch here?"

"I don't know." Joy stared morosely into her teacup. "I only came to see if you'd heard from Paul."

"Now why in the blazes would *I* hear from Paul?" her mother exclaimed with patent exasperation. "Seems to me, if you wanted to keep track of him, you should have kept him with you!"

Marie didn't even pretend to be happy with her daughter right now and made no bones about the fact that she thought Joy's actions with regard to Paul reprehensible.

"Once having married the man, why couldn't you at least have tried to make a decent go of it? You think people are talking now? Wait till they find out you're not even living together!"

Thoroughly disgruntled, Marie loudly banged her pots.

Weary—did her mother think she *enjoyed* the mess in which she found herself?—Joy propped an elbow on the table and put her head in her hand.

She was all mixed-up, was the problem. She no longer knew what was right and what was wrong, what was real and what was fantasy. Where Paul Mallik and herself were concerned, nothing was as it seemed or even as it should have been.

She had saved a man from drowning and now look at her. Something like two weeks later and she was drowning herself. Drowning in misery. And married to a man who had wed her out of a sense of chivalry and gratitude, but, nevertheless, under duress.

What had his first reaction been? *Never. No, sir. Not ever.*

Remembering, Joy winced. She pinched the bridge of her nose. "I've got a headache."

"Go take some aspirin," her mother said curtly.

Joy dropped her hand with a sigh. Even her mother hated her. Or, at the least, didn't like her much right now. Paul probably hated her for sure.

On her way to the bathroom and some aspirin, Joy stopped in her tracks as a devastating thought struck her. The *Explorer II* had sailed this morning.

What if Paul had gone back on board ship and sailed out of her life for good?

# Chapter Nine

That afternoon, Joy stayed in her classroom long after the children and her colleagues had gone home. She supposed she should go to her apartment and do some more packing up, maybe run a load over to the cottage. But she couldn't quite rouse herself to do either.

She considered going back to her mother's, but decided she had done more than her share of running back to Mom lately. It was time she took charge of her own self again.

All right. Joy pulled her handbag out of her desk drawer and stood up. She had done all the catch-up and busywork she could here. It was late. Almost eight o'clock, in fact. Too late for church choir practice, had she been in the mood to attend it.

Not that they would have been expecting her to. As far as everyone in town was concerned, she and Paul were on their honeymoon, even if work and such had made it impossible for them to take a trip.

Which made bumping into Sheila MacKenzie—no, *Harris* now, of course—and Lorraine Seifert, both life-long friends of Joy's and members of the same church choir, doubly embarrassing for Joy.

It was on the sidewalk in front of the convenience store. Joy had stopped on her way home to pick up some milk and cereal since the cupboards at her apartment were so appallingly bare. Not that she needed much, her appetite was nil these days, but she had sense enough to know she needed *something* in the morning in order to function at work.

In her depressed state of mind, Joy had completely forgotten that Luigi's Pizza Place, next door to the convenience store, was where the choir members went to grab a bite after practice. As she got out of her car, a group of them were exiting Luigi's.

Sheila, just back from her own brief honeymoon with Vernon, spotted Joy and made a big to-do out of greeting her. Naturally, some of the others stopped, as well. Aside from the fact that Joy had become somewhat notorious by virtue of her publicly proclaimed pregnancy and rather hush-hush marriage to a complete stranger—whom nobody had met or even laid eyes on!—the prospect of witnessing a confrontation between the two rivals for Vernon Harris's favor was too good to pass up.

And so they hovered discreetly in the background as they eagerly watched this meeting of Joy and Sheila, who kept a visibly white-knuckled grip on Lorraine Seifert's sleeve as if to keep her from fading into the background, too.

Afraid to face me alone, the two-faced, cowardly little man snatcher, Joy thought venomously as she returned the other woman's too-sweet smile with one of her own.

"I hear congratulations are in order," Sheila drawled, arching a brow as she flicked a pointed glance at Joy's slender midriff. She spoke loud enough to be heard across the street.

Joy clenched her back teeth, raised her chin a fraction and kept her smile rigidly in place. She felt it beneath her to toss back a comment about Sheila's precipitous pregnancy.

"A husband *and* a baby—" Sheila continued, including everyone around in her meaningful glance. "My, my. What a fast worker you've become, Joy Marie."

Joy ignored her, addressing Lorraine instead. The woman looked decidedly uncomfortable and tried repeatedly, and in vain, to disengage herself from Sheila's grip.

"How's Frank and little Sara?" Joy asked her. "Over the flu, I hope?"

"Oh, sure." Lorraine once again tugged at Sheila's sleeve. "Thanks for asking, but they're fine—"

"We missed you at choir practice, Joy Marie," Sheila broke in. "Not that we didn't understand, right, everybody? Joy's still on her honeymoon, after all. So, uh..."

Her glittering gaze swept the surrounding area. "...where is the lucky man? Paul Mallik, isn't that what he's called? I'm sure we'd all just *love* to meet him."

Aside from Sheila's catty titter, a few others could be heard, as well. Joy wished the ground would open up and swallow her or, failing that, that she were the kind of woman who engaged in public catfights. She would dearly love to hurl herself at Vernon Harris's new bride and yank her red hair out by its mousy brown roots.

"Someone mention my name?"

Every bit as shocked as everyone else apparently was, Joy whirled toward the sound of Paul's voice just as he stepped onto the sidewalk next to her.

"Sorry to keep you waiting, darling," he said, putting a proprietary arm around Joy and pulling her flush against his side. Numb with shock as she was, she could only stare at him as he bent his head and pressed a soft kiss onto her lips. "I got here before you and went into the hardware store for a minute. So..."

He looked at the assembled group with an inquisitively amiable smile. "Friends of yours?"

"Uh—" Thoroughly rattled—where had he come from? Had he always been this handsome? This tall? This self-assured?—Joy couldn't think of a thing to say. All she knew was that whatever debt Paul might think he owed her—and there wasn't one, as far as she was concerned—he had just paid it. In full and then some.

He must have felt her tremble, because his hold tightened as he extended a hand to Sheila, who was unabashedly staring. He introduced himself. "I'm Paul." And, raising a brow when she didn't immediately respond, added, "And you are...?"

"Sh-Sheila, uh, Harris," Sheila stammered, releasing Lorraine's sleeve to gingerly take Paul's hand. "And this is—"

"Lorraine Seifert," Lorraine interrupted with a genuine smile. She had always been a good friend of Joy's, but of Sheila's, as well. She'd been caught in the middle of her friends' difficulties and was clearly relieved to see Joy so obviously well married. "I'm sure I speak for all of us when I say, welcome to the community, Mr. Mallik."

"Paul." Paul's smile, Joy realized with a jolt akin to a punch in the stomach, could have charmed the birds out of their trees.

"Joy and I were about to get a bite to eat," Paul said, startling Joy with his urbanity and smooth manner. "If you'd care to join us...?"

He glanced invitingly around while Joy, inwardly bouncing from shock to shock, recoiled in horror. To her relief, no one seemed inclined to accept Paul's invitation, though Lorraine clearly voiced everyone's sentiments when she said, "We'll take a rain check, if you don't mind, and give you two honeymooners some privacy.

"Wonderful meeting you, Paul," she said, and now she was the one who gripped her friend's sleeve and hauled her away with a warm "All the best, Joy Marie" to Joy, which the rest of the chorus echoed.

As soon as the group was out of earshot, Joy went limp. Her knees shook in reaction and, turning to Paul, she sagged against him.

"Oh, Paul." Her head dropped to his shoulder. She was trembling all over.

"It's all right." Angry with her though he was, Paul's heart went out to her. Poor impulsive Joy, he thought, bringing his other arm around and holding her while she fought to collect her shattered composure. Little had she known what she would get herself into by insisting on this bizarre marriage of theirs. "They're gone now. You can relax. Come on."

Cupping Joy's chin, he raised her head so that she had to look at him. "Let's go inside."

"No." The very thought of facing some more of the townfolk brought nausea into Joy's throat. "I, uh, I already ate at Ma's. I'm not hungry."

"Well, I am," Paul said. "So have a glass of wine and keep me company while I eat."

"There'll be others there," Joy objected, certain she was not up to another confrontation such as she'd just endured. "They'll stare at us."

"So let them stare. I don't mind. Besides," Paul challenged as some of his hurt and disillusionment broke through the shackles of his iron control, "this is what you wanted a stand-in husband for, isn't it? For the town to see you? With me? To prove to them and that old boyfriend of yours how desirable I find you, what a catch he gave up? So come on—"

Almost roughly, he spun her around and, keeping one arm clamped around her shoulders, marched her into the restaurant. "—here's your chance. Let me show them how crazy I am about you. Let them see what a stud I am, to have gotten you pregnant in just two days."

"Paul..."

Joy was appalled by the emotion that vibrated in his tone. Why, he sounded angry at her, she realized with dismay. Angry and disgusted with the role in which she had cast him for her benefit. Her vanity.

And in that instant it hit her, what she had done. To salvage her excessive pride and by publicly proclaiming herself pregnant—and she'd known full well that anything said in front of Mike Jessup might as well have been announced by the town crier—she had taken away Paul's pride. Paul's autonomy. She had backed him into a corner from which he could not possibly have emerged with his honor intact.

Whether he married her or not, her family and the good folk of Seacrest would think him an oversexed adventurer who repaid the woman who'd saved his life by ravishing her.

Oh, good Lord. Mortification bathed Joy in a hot
flame of red. What had she done? To him? To herself?
How could she face anyone? How could *he?*

"No." She dug in her heels to keep him from taking
her into Luigi's but she was no match for his strength.
Still she struggled. "Paul, wait.... This is all so terrible.
So wrong..."

"Is it?" He stopped then, no more than a foot from
the restaurant front door.

"Yes," Joy cried, gripping his arms in her urgency. "I
just realized... Oh, Paul, I'm so sorry. What have I
done? What must these people think of us? Of—of
you...?"

Paul endured her emotional outburst with outward
stoicism. "A little late in the day to be worrying about
what people think, *Mrs. Mallik,* isn't it?"

Paul's emotions with regard to Joy had run the gamut
since the night of their wedding when she'd so callously
denied him entry into her apartment. And thus into her
life. As far as he was concerned, she had reduced their
marriage of mutual convenience to its basest form and
cast each of them into the role of common, cold-blooded
user.

So be it. Though the role into which she had cast him
was an insult to him and his integrity, he had put it behind him and gone on with the business of coming to
grips with the situation in which he found himself—a not-
really married man in a foreign country.

Part of him resented and, in the loneliness of night,
even hated Joy for what she'd done, but another part
recognized and appreciated the gift he'd been given. The
opportunity to leave Gorska and the pain of his memories, and the chance to make a life for himself in the

country of his dreams. It was for this that he owed Joy a debt.

Tonight he had been handed an opportunity to repay this debt, to at least pay part of it, by coming to Joy's aid out here on this sidewalk. But there was more to be done. The drama, once staged, had to be acted out to its logical conclusion. He and Joy, the stars of this piece, had yet to give the audience their money's worth.

They would do that tonight at Luigi's. They would act their roles as star-crossed lovers whether his *wife* felt up to the part or not. She owed him that. Owed him the chance to cancel his debt and be done with it. And with her.

"Never forget that *you* wanted this, *carsya mu*," he said, his tone making a mockery of the Gorskan endearment which translated meant, my little bird. "You wanted your pound of flesh so, by all means, let's go collect it from them and be done."

Ignoring Joy's wretchedness, he ushered her into the restaurant. Exiting patrons made it impossible for Joy to openly object or resist without creating more of a spectacle than they likely had already. All through the confrontation with Sheila and the others, Joy had been excruciatingly aware of the fascinated spectators inside Luigi's who'd been fortunate enough to have window seats.

"Two," Paul told the hostess, Nancy Tompkins whose mother was a close friend of Marie Cooper.

"Smoking or non?" Marie asked with a melting glance and flirty smile at Paul that set Joy's teeth on edge. She could just imagine the field day Nancy was going to have spreading the word that she had actually seated Joy and her mysterious *husband*. Now where could Joy have found such a hunk? On the beach? Ha-ha...!

"Non," Paul said, flashing the heart-stopping smile Joy hadn't even known he possessed until a few minutes ago out on that sidewalk.

Where was the drawn and haggard merman she had rescued from the sea? Whom she had had to dress and feed like a baby? Who'd been sad and confused, lost and needy?

Joy asked herself those questions with something like desperation as she followed Nancy to their table. And all the while she was painfully aware not only of Paul's imposing presence close behind her, but of dozens of pairs of eyes following their progress. Speculating eyes that avoided hers as she passed in Nancy's wake and with her husband in tow. Eyes that tried and judged them based solely on what they saw. Or, more likely, on what they wanted to see.

And suddenly Joy thought, To hell with them. She couldn't believe she'd been so shallow as to care what they thought of her being abandoned by Vern. Those who knew her well, those who truly cared, had sympathized with her. And those others, with their phony empathy and their whispers behind her back? Who cared what they thought? Then, or now?

Feeling as if a weight had been lifted off her shoulders, Joy turned to give Paul a dazzlingly happy smile. She would explain her belated insights later, she thought and, seeing his eyes widen with something like shock in response to her smile, reached back to take his hand.

Paul, thinking this was part of the act, that for some reason Joy felt the time had come to get into the role of happily newlywed bride, only spared a moment of regret for the waste of such a beautiful smile. He caught her hand in his and his gaze delved into hers with what he hoped was convincing ardor.

*"Trusora,"* he murmured in something like a stage whisper, tugging on Joy's hand to stay her while he caught up with her and clasped her around the waist. He nuzzled her temple, the silk of her hair and knew with a sharp stab of regret that he'd give quite a lot to have this scene be real.

*Trusora* he'd called her, the Gorskan word for treasure, which was a term of endearment, as well. And a treasure Joy was.

Or could be, Paul amended with a profound sense of regret, if only she would recognize the futility of trying to influence public opinion and learn to only be true to herself.

Her hair smelled like the sun-kissed meadows in which he'd romped as a boy. It had the texture of silk, the color of flax, the abundance of sheaves of ripe wheat.

Paul inhaled sharply, audibly, bringing Joy's head around like a startled doe's.

"What?" she murmured, her eyes wide and aware.

"You," Paul whispered, forgetting for a moment that they were but actors on a stage. He nuzzled her ear, dropped a kiss at her temple. "Just...you..."

Joy thought her heart would surely stand still. Paul's lips at her temple were soft as velvet, his voice a silken caress.

And the word, that one, single, pulsating word he'd uttered, "You..." rang on in her soul, as sweet and enduring as an angel's hosanna.

"Paul." All of her newfound humility, all of her insight, her regret over done deeds that she longed to undo, Joy instilled in the name that fell from her lips in one tremulous sigh. There was so much she wanted to say to him, so much she now knew to be true. There were thoughts she needed to share with him. And feelings...

Lord—such huge and wondrous feelings.

Gazing into Paul's eyes, Joy was sure he knew most of those feelings already. There was only the two of them; the world had spun away....

"Hey, Paul! Sis!"

With matching expressions of shock and awakening, Paul and Joy turned their heads toward the sound of Ernie Cooper's voice.

He was beaming at them from a large corner table—Jolene, as well as Mike and Karen Jessup were there with him, too. He was waving his beefy arm, beckoning them to come.

"You lovebirds get over here," he hollered. "C'mon...!"

After exchanging startled glances with Nancy Tompkins, Joy and Paul, both working at producing pleased grins, made their way to Ernie's table.

Paul had reared away from Joy at the sound of Ernie's voice and, though he'd kept hold of her hand, Joy felt as bereft as if he'd walked out the door and left her. Which he had in a way because his emotional withdrawal, too, was to Joy a tangible thing.

Joy sensed—no, she *knew* with all the certainty of her woman's intuition—that Paul had forgotten the strain between them for a little while there, just as she had.

But she also knew that now it was back, and in spades, though he continued to play the role of affectionate bridegroom to the hilt.

The whole town would know now, as Paul and Joy joined the boisterous group at Ernie's table, that the Cooper family was behind Joy Marie's choice of a husband all the way.

By Ernie inviting them to his table, by his calling Paul by name and dubbing the couple "lovebirds," the seal of approval had officially been given. The show, for all intents and purposes, was over and every customer in Luigi's sighed a sigh of regret for the drama they'd hoped to witness but hadn't.

And then Vern and Sheila Harris walked in.

Later, back out on the sidewalk with Paul, after taking their leave from Ernie and his gang, Joy was still convinced Sheila had hurried home and dragged Vern back to Luigi's for the sole purpose of giving Joy some embarassing moments.

Well, if so, Joy was pleased to know the little hussy's plan had backfired. Rather than be embarrassed, Joy had reveled in the knowledge that hers was the vastly more handsome, sophisticated and sexy of the two men, and she had shamelessly played the role of adoring bride to the hilt.

If Paul had seemed reticent, and if Ernie and Jolene had seemed to exchange a troubled gaze or two, Joy hadn't cared. Everything had turned out the way she'd fantasized it would when Vernon had dumped her. Only better.

"Oh, Vern honey, come say hi to Joy Marie's *husband*," Sheila had cooed, dragging her scowling, and obviously reluctant, spouse over to Ernie's table where she took charge of the introductions, too. "Vern honey, this is Paul—it was Paul, wasn't it? Yes? Well, meet *my* husband, Vernon Harris. We're all just real old friends of Joy Marie's," she added as the two men stiffly shook hands. "And so gosh darn happy she's finally found a man of her own."

Joy had known full well, of course, that that last remark meant to infer that prior to Paul's appearance on the scene, Joy had been pursuing men who belonged to other women. Specifically, Vernon Harris whom Sheila very much considered private property.

Ha! With her hand warmly clasped in Paul's, with his thigh intimately pressed against hers in the confines of their booth and Ernie's reassuring bulk bracketing her on the left, Joy felt smug enough to inwardly sneer at Sheila Harris's naïveté. The day that Vernon Harris would be faithful to one woman would be the day he was dead.

Looking at him, noting for the first time that some of his muscle had begun to turn to fat, comparing him with Paul, Joy wondered what she'd ever seen in her ex-fiancé. And she realized that a lot of his attraction had been a carryover from their high school days when he'd been the jock all the girls had panted after.

She had reveled in the fact that he had chosen *her* as his steady even though she hadn't been as free with her favors as—according to Vern, of course—some of her friends were willing to be. Being seen in Vernon's car, being singled out by him, rushed by him, had been an enormous source of pride to Joy.

Pride. Joy was too elated tonight to spare that particular affliction of hers, and her mother's edict that pride goeth before the fall, more than a quick, rueful thought. She'd fallen, all right, but she'd picked herself up, hadn't she? Picked herself up and gone on to better things. A better man....

Standing on the sidewalk in front of Luigi's, her arm linked with Paul's while they waved goodbye to Ernie and Jolene, Joy was blissfully sure that everything had worked itself out for the best.

"What a wonderful evening." With a sigh and a dreamy smile, she turned to Paul. "Your place or mine?" she murmured, playfully tiptoeing her fingers up his arm to his impressive biceps. "Not that you've told me yet where your place is."

It took her a moment to realize that Paul no longer shared her loverlike mood. He was scowling, in fact, while gently, but very pointedly, removing her fingers from his arm.

"I believe it is nearly midnight," he murmured. "And, if my memory of the fairy tale serves me right, it is time for Cinderella to return to her coach lest it turn into a pumpkin."

"Cinderella?" Joy stared at him, bewildered. "What're you talking about?"

"Me," Paul said. He indicated the now-darkened restaurant—their group had been the last to leave—with an inclination of his head. "The party's over, my friend. It's time I went back to being who I really am. And," he said, brushing a kiss across Joy's brow before taking a step back and away from her, "so should you."

He took another backward step and another while Joy, dumbstruck and immobilized by this unexpected turn of events, only stood there.

"Goodbye, *carsya mu,*" he said softly, almost sadly, pivoting with a wave of his hand.

And then, as Joy stood and listened inside of herself to the sound of her heart breaking, he trotted over to a Jeep Cherokee, all shiny and new, hopped in and, moments later, roared off into the night.

Joy watched the Jeep's taillights disappear around a corner, listened to the ever-weakening roar of its engine until it had faded to naught. And still she stood on that sidewalk, now deserted. The town was quiet; only the ocean's faint roar could be heard above the leaden beat of her heart.

"Everything okay, Joy Marie?"

"What?" Dazed, Joy turned her head toward Howard Cheng, owner and chief chef of Luigi's Pizza Place. He was locking the door and eyeing her with concern.

"You okay?" he asked again.

"Wha— Oh, sure. Sure, Howie." With a small shake of the head, Joy collected herself. She even managed a little laugh. "I'm fine. Just...ozoning here for a minute."

"Nice guy, your husband." Howard stowed his keys and prepared to head up the street to his house, a few blocks away. "Where'd he get to?"

"Oh." Joy shrugged, vaguely indicating her car, still parked at the curb. "He's, uh, gone ahead home. We, uh, came in separate cars. You know..."

"Oh, sure. Well." Howard waved a jaunty good-night. "Have a good one."

"You, too." Joy stared after him for a moment and then, every step as heavy as if she were dragging a ball and chain, she went to her car and got in.

She didn't start the engine right away, only sat there, contemplating the emptiness she felt inside. She shook her head in disbelief and asked herself how she could have lost sight of the fact that she and Paul had only been putting on an act tonight in that restaurant.

Oh, God... Had she made a fool of herself in there? In front of the others?

With a groan, Joy pressed her palms against her scalding cheeks and closed her eyes on the image of herself the way she'd been—smugly superior to the Harrises, and with everyone else flirtatious, vivacious, witty and warm.

All of that or...just plain silly?

Joy bit her lip, humiliation making her want to cringe and hide. But there wasn't anyone to hide *from*, was there? She was alone. Alone and, suddenly, so very, very lonely.

As always when she needed a place to lick her wounds, Joy put her car in gear and headed for the cottage.

# Chapter Ten

At first, Joy didn't know to whom the gleaming Jeep Cherokee that was parked in the cottage carport belonged. Or, indeed, where she had seen it before. Because she *had* seen it before. But it didn't take her more than a moment—a moment at once daunting and exhilarating—to figure it out.

It was Paul's. Paul was here. Here, at *her* beach house. So this was where he'd gone to live.

Joy's spirits soared. Her heart lifted. It tossed off its lethargy and launched into a lively gallop.

She turned off the engine of her car and jumped out, all set to run into the house and greet her husband with a glad cry.

But then she thought, Wait a minute. Where did Paul Mallik get off putting her through hell wondering where he was, when all the time he was sitting fat and happy in *her* beach house? And without so much as a "by your leave," too. How dare he?

Suddenly furious—he might have told her tonight at Luigi's where he lived, mightn't he? And where the hell had he gotten the key from, she'd like to know—Joy marched up to the back door and slammed it open.

"Paul Mallik!" she called. "You come out here right now or I'll have you arrested for breaking and entering!" An empty threat, but she thought it sounded good.

She crossed the porch and stomped into the kitchen. And came to a dead stop. "Ernie!" Her keychain dropped out of her hand.

"Hi, sis." Ernie, without looking up from whatever it was he was doing, absently saluted her with a can of pop.

Catercorner across from him at the kitchen table sat Paul. His expression at seeing her was a mixture of surprise and wariness. Some sheets of square ruled paper, several pencils and a ruler were scattered on the table between the men.

"I's just giving your husband some pointers about that new carport you're always yammering about," Ernie growled. "Give us a minute, will ya."

Joy couldn't believe it. Bent over the paper with their heads together, the men looked like bosom buddies who worked together all the time. As if this were just another day in the life of the Coopers and the Malliks.

"B-but, Ernie... where's your car?" Joy stammered. From the thousand and one questions that crowded her mind, that was the one that fell from her tongue.

"Other side of the house." Ernie didn't look up from what he was doing.

"B-but... Jolene...?"

"Got a ride with the Jessups. Look, sis—" Ernie finally raised his head, but only to scowl at her "—do you mind? We're trying to figure something out here."

He resumed his task, leaving Joy to stand there, at a loss.

"Close your mouth, sis," Ernie said. "And close the back door, too, while you're at it. There's a draft."

She almost hit him then. Would have, if underneath all her inward fuming and bewildered stutterings she hadn't been so darned glad to have found Paul again.

Not that Paul needed to know she was glad. She had plenty of reasons to be mad at him. But Ernie. When did those two get as thick as thieves?

Hey. Something dawned on her. Ernie probably thought she lived here *with* Paul. She hadn't talked to him since Sunday morning; he didn't know that she'd been frantically trying to locate Paul and make amends for her rash rejection of him on their wedding night.

That had to be it! Ernie thought everything between her and Paul was hunky-dory. Which would explain why he had hailed them so cordially at Luigi's tonight, too.

And Paul hadn't told him otherwise.

Joy stared at Paul with a surge of affectionate gratitude. He glanced up from Ernie's scribbles just then and caught her gaze. His own turned from wary to quizzical and, as their eye contact lengthened, darkened with something intangible, but, to Joy, immeasurably warming.

Until Ernie growled, "Are you paying attention here, Mallik?"

"Of course." With a rueful half grin, Paul refocused on Ernie's sheet of paper.

Joy brushed a hand across her brow in bewilderment. She was such a mass of emotions inside. It had been such a long and eventful day. A day that had, it seemed to her, been one long emotional roller-coaster ride.

She had known real despair when she hadn't been able to find out Paul's whereabouts. And when she'd thought he might have gone back to sea. Even now that thought made her heart plummet to the pit of her stomach.

The wildest kind of joy had filled her when Paul, as if by magic, had turned up next to her in front of Luigi's. In front of her "friends." None of whom would ever again have reason to doubt that Joy Marie Cooper's brand-new husband was anything but nuts about her. Lord, what a triumph!

But a triumph that had proved to be shallow, not to mention all too fleeting, when Paul had taken his leave from her again out on that sidewalk.

And now this. Another peak of happiness, the highest yet. To find him here. Here, where it had all begun. To see him sitting here in her kitchen, calmly talking carports with her brother.

Didn't that suggest he planned to stay in her life? For the next little while, at least? Perhaps long enough to give her a chance to... What? Love him?

She already did.

Joy abruptly turned her back on the men, lest she betray the revelation that had just come to her. She was sure it was written all over her face and she didn't want it to be broadcast in this way. She wanted to savor the feeling, hug the knowledge to her heart while she waited for the right time. For some special moment when she would be sure that Paul wanted it. Wanted her. Without feeling trapped.

"I, uh, forgot something in the car," she muttered to no one in particular and swiftly walked from the room.

Outside, gazing up at the sky, it seemed like every star in the universe had gathered overhead. Without city lights to dilute their brilliance, they sparkled like millions of diamonds scattered across a spread of black velvet.

*Star light, star bright . . .*

Did they? Would they?

Joy pressed a hand to her heart, closed her eyes and wished with all the power of her being for a chance to show Paul Mallik that she loved him.

"Penny for your thoughts." As if conjured up by her fervent concentration, Paul materialized at Joy's side. "Isn't that what they say?"

"Yes." Joy opened her eyes but otherwise didn't dare move for fear he might evaporate like a genie back into some mythical bottle. "Has Ernie left?"

"Yes, by the front door. He said to tell you good-night."

In the silence that followed, they both gazed up at the heavens.

"I was thinking that I've never seen the stars so bright," Joy said softly.

"They *are* beautiful." But Paul's eyes were on Joy now, not on the stars. "As you are, *carsya*."

"Don't," Joy said with a forced little laugh. "Cinderella time, remember?"

"I was wrong to say that." Paul shoved his hands into his back pockets to keep from touching her. He had hurt her out there on that sidewalk. It had cut him like a knife to realize that he had. "I was angry."

"And you had every right to be," Joy whispered. "I, uh, crossed the line. I wanted—"

"Yes, and I, too, wanted," Paul cut in with suppressed violence. "Things I found out I couldn't have. Things you were not willing to give in this marriage we made. You allowed me a glimpse, a taste of something, someone, that I—"

With effort, Paul reigned in his emotions. "For a little while," he said in a quieter, tired voice, "in that restaurant tonight, I lost sight of our... agreement. I'm sorry."

Not nearly as sorry as she had been, Joy thought, hugging herself against the shivers that racked her, though not from cold. *Tell him,* a voice inside her urged. *Speak to him. For once, be completely open with him.*

"I've been looking for you," she said. "Ever since yesterday evening."

"You have?" Joy seemed different to Paul tonight, out here. Different from the headstrong, never-take-no-for-an-answer, I'll-show-'em young woman who in just a few short days had managed to irrevocably change the course of his life. She seemed softer, uncertain. "Why?"

Joy hugged herself more tightly. "I also wanted to say I'm sorry. And that I..."

She swallowed, her constricted throat making it difficult for her to speak. "That I wouldn't blame you if you hated me."

"Hated you? Ah, *carsya...*" Gently, Paul laid his palm against her cheek. Another shiver trembled through Joy at his touch. Paul urged her face around to his. "What nonsense is this, then, hmm?"

His hand dropped from Joy's face to her shoulder and he drew her toward him.

"How could I hate you?" he murmured. "You gave me back my life as well as the chance for a whole new existence in a place I could only dream of before. Hate you? If I live to be a hundred, I'll never be able to repay you for what you have done."

He drew back a little and pressed a kiss on her forehead. "So do not be sorry, my little Samaritan. For I am not."

"You're not?" Oh, but it was wonderful to be in his arms, even when he only meant to comfort her.

"I'm not," Paul repeated earnestly, giving her shoulders a little squeeze before he released her.

Joy mourned the loss of his warmth. She cast around for something to say. "I, uh, I'll be moving in here on Wednesday. Did, um, Ernie tell you?"

"No." Surprise, pleasure, heat—Paul took a deep breath. "No, he didn't." He cleared his throat. "Do you mind my living here, too? Only until I—?"

"No," Joy said quickly. "No, of course not. Stay as long as you want. I—that is, if you don't mind that I...?"

"Mind?" Paul raked a hand through his hair. Given their arrangement and the state of his emotions, it would kill him, that's all. "How could I mind? This is your house. I'm grateful—"

Joy didn't know why; perhaps her emotions had been buffeted once too often today. But at his offhand tone and attitude, something snapped.

"Will you *stop* being so damned grateful all the time!" she erupted, flinging her hands up in the air. "I am sick of it. Sick of all this pussyfooting around, sick of being so careful to say the right thing all the time. It's driving me crazy. *You're* driving me crazy!"

"And do you think you're not driving *me* crazy, too?" Paul, too, had been pushed too far. "Do you think I feel nothing? Want nothing? Am nothing? That I have no pride?"

"I never said—"

"You're *always* talking, that's your problem!" Roughly, Paul caught Joy's arm and hauled her against him.

"Always talking?" Furious, Joy twisted free. "Well, I won't be talking to you again anytime soon. I'm leaving."

"Running is more like it," Paul snarled. "Whenever things don't go your way, that's your solution, isn't it, Joy Marie?"

The arrow struck home with a vengeance. With a choked "Leave me alone!" Joy ran to her car.

She had almost reached it when Paul called, "Don't go!"

Joy's steps faltered. She was hurt, and furious with him. Because what he'd said about running was true?

She stopped, but didn't turn around.

"I'm sorry, *carsya.*" Paul came up behind her and put his hands on her shoulders.

As always, his touch had the power to thrill. Joy flinched.

Paul snatched back his hands and took a step back.

Afraid he had misconstrued her reaction, Joy quickly turned around.

"Paul...?" The quiver in her voice betrayed her weakness, her longing, but Joy no longer cared. The dim bulb on the post by the carport illuminated Paul's face sufficiently for her to see the lines of strain there, the haunted expression.

"Don't go," he said again.

"Oh, Paul." Fed up with words, Joy rose up on her toes and kissed him.

The soft and tentative pressure of Joy's trembling lips hit every nerve in Paul's tension-filled body with the force of a high-voltage charge. With a violent tremor and a groan that got lost in Joy's mouth, his arms closed around her slender form in an embrace so fervent, it lifted Joy clear off her feet.

All of his need, his longing, all of the desperate hunger that came from having returned from the brink of death, culminated in a kiss so raw, so primitive and wild, it threatened to devour them both.

Joy's hands fell away from Paul's face to clasp his neck. Paul swung her up in his arms. Without breaking the kiss, he carried her into the house, through the kitchen and to the room where he slept.

But on the threshold he stopped. A measure of sanity returned. *Be sure,* something whispered. *Be sure.*

He raised his head, and, freeing one hand, flipped the wall switch. The overhead light came on, bathing the room in brightness.

Unwelcome brightness, as far as Joy was concerned. She blinked and quickly closed her eyes again. "Please turn it off."

Her lips formed the words with delicious awkwardness. They were swollen from the mindless ferocity of their soul-shattering kisses.

"No, *trusora.*" Paul's voice was husky, rich and warm like the rarest cognac and, to Joy, every bit as intoxicating.

"I need you to be sure," Paul said. "As sure as I am. I want you to look at me, to really see me. I want to be sure you know who it is with whom you make love."

"I don't need to see you to know." Joy protested.

"Yes, you do." A hint of command put an edge in Paul's voice. "Open your eyes, *carsya mu.* Look well. And be sure that you know it is not your Vernon Harris—"

"What?" If Paul had dropped Joy naked into a snowbank, he could not have more effectively cooled her off. "Vernon Harris! Oh, what a rotten thing to say!"

Furious with him, and near tears with frustration and disappointment, Joy struggled out of Paul's arms. "I don't care one whit about Vernon Harris."

"Oh, really?" Had this bitterness he felt been there all along? Paul wondered. This...jealousy? And he snarled, "When *he* is the only reason you married me?"

"He is not the only reason and you damned well know it!" Joy straightened her clothes with shaking hands. "You'd probably be in the middle of the Pacific somewhere, steaming toward some godforsaken dot on the map if not for this marriage!"

"Yes, and probably better off!" Paul slammed the flat of his hand against the wall, making the pictures there list to port.

"Well!" That did it. She was out of here.

Her head high but her temper higher still, Joy rushed past him out of the room, out of the house and into her car.

Only to discover there that she didn't have her keys.

"Oh, damn." Her fists pounded the steering wheel. Damn, damn, damn...

Paul knocked on the driver's-side window.

Joy's head whipped around.

Paul held up his hand, her keychain dangling from one finger.

Her motions jerky, Joy rolled down the window. "Give me those." She made a grab for them.

Paul jerked his hand out of range. "Not until you let me apologize."

"Don't bother."

"I insist." He leaned down, his expression troubled. "I don't want to fight with you, *carsya mu.*"

"Then why do you?"

"There are things between us—"

"Things like Vernon Harris?"

"Joy..." How to tell her that he was racked with jealousy of that man? He couldn't.

And so, lamely, inadequately, he said, "I'm very sorry."

Joy jerked her eyes toward the front, blinking rapidly. "Okay, fine."

Paul's lips thinned. He stayed as he was for another moment, then, when Joy only continued to stare straight ahead, with a sigh, he straightened and dropped the keys into her lap.

"Perhaps," he said heavily, "everything considered, it is better this way."

"No doubt." Her fingers shaking, Joy fumbled the key into the ignition and turned it. The engine sprang to life and she slammed the gear into Reverse. "Let me tell you this, though, Mr. High-and-mighty Mallik, at least *I* don't go around calling the person I kiss the breath out of, *Anna!*"

And with that Joy floored the gas pedal and shot out of the driveway as if she were driving in the Indy.

"Joy..." Rosa Mertz, the principal, tiptoed into Joy's classroom.

The kids were working on an art project for Mother's Day. At a sign from Joy, they chorused, "Good morning, Mrs. Mertz."

"Good morning, children. As you were." Rosa, beaming, turned to Joy. "You do such a good job with them."

Joy smiled her thanks, a little wanly. She didn't feel particularly deserving of praise today.

Rosa lowered her voice. "Are you still planning to take your class on that field trip to Haystack Rock?"

"What? Oh." So distracted was Joy—still reeling from
the fiasco with Paul Mallik last night—that it took her a
moment to get a grip on what Rosa was talking about.
"Haystack Rock, yes. Let me see now..."

She flipped through her lesson planner with no real
purpose except to gather her thoughts.

"Because if you are," Rosa continued, "there's a really good minus tide the next couple of days. And Sally
Jenkins is interested in making it a combined outing with
her fourth graders."

Joy nodded. "Sounds good to me."

"And she had what I thought was a wonderful idea,
too." Rosa paused expectantly.

Joy glanced up. "Oh?"

"Yes." Rosa's eyes gleamed with suppressed excite-
ment. She spoke very slowly at first and then picked up
speed. "How about you ask your husband to come along
and instruct the kids on all the exposed sea life we're
bound to see? Since he is a marine biologist."

Oh my gosh. Joy strained to find another smile. This
was terrible. It was a wonderful idea, but this was terrible. Because how could she ask Paul such a thing when
she had vowed never to speak to the man again?

"Umm..." She bit her lip.

Rosa, visibly disappointed, arched her brows. "You
don't think he'd want to do it?"

"Oh, no." Joy gave herself a little shake. "I'm sure
he'd be very glad to do it. It's just—well, which day did
you and, uh, Sally have in mind? I, that is, we are going
to be moving tomorrow.

"Into the cottage," she elaborated. Everyone knew she
had inherited her grandmother's beach house some time
ago.

"How nice," Rosa said with a smile. "Apartments are so confining, aren't they, with a man around?"

Joy nodded, though she didn't doubt that the beach house was bound to be just as confining when the man in question was Paul Mallik. In fact, she would probably be aware of—and bothered by—him if they cohabited in a place the size of Grand Central Station.

"How about Thursday then," Rosa suggested. "Would that work for you?"

"Well, I'd have to check with, uh, Paul, of course...."

"Of course." Rosa patted her on the shoulder. "And if he can't, well, we'll just have to muddle through on our own. But you *will* try to convince him, won't you?"

"Of course."

Ernie called Joy at the school at lunchtime. It was one of those one-sided telephone conversations that were his style.

"Change of plan, sis," he announced without preamble. "We're moving you today. Den's got something on for tomorrow and my truck's gotta go in for service before me and Jolene take the kids camping this weekend. Don't worry about a thing, though—Paul's already at the apartment packing everything up. It'll all be over, 'cept for some cleaning, time you get off work. Bye."

Needless to say, her pupils spent a lot of time on their art project that afternoon. Their teacher was in no condition to tackle advanced multiplication or simple fractions.

All she could think of was that she would be sleeping at the cottage tonight. One night sooner than planned. And one night later than—for some wild and reckless moments—she had hoped.

* * *

The apartment was spick-and-span. There was no reason to hang around any longer, but Joy checked every room one more time with weary satisfaction. Whatever other stories old Edna might find to spread about Joy, she would never have reason to call her a slob.

Joy had gone to the apartment straight from school. She always kept some sweats in her locker there and, rather than go home—and face Paul—to change, had opted to slip into those. She had borrowed the cleaning utensils from her mother who had blessedly been away at her bridge club.

Unable to detect even one last speck of dust, and equally unable to come up with any other delaying tactics, Joy reluctantly admitted it was time to go home to the beach house. A lot of work would be waiting there for her, too. Unpacking, as well as finding a place for everything. Though Ernie would be storing most of the large pieces of furniture in a corner of the stevedoring warehouse until Joy decided what she wanted to do with it all, there were tons of little items to be incorporated into the cottage household.

If she kept busy enough, she probably wouldn't even have to speak to Paul, beyond the courtesies.

Driving down the narrow road that branched off the highway toward the beach house, Joy half hoped that his Jeep Cherokee would be gone. No such luck. Paul had parked it off to the side, though, leaving the soon-to-be-refurbished carport free to shelter Joy's modest compact.

Joy was touched by Paul's thoughtfulness, but irritated by it, too. It made staying angry with him a lot more difficult.

Walking into the house and finding dinner waiting for her made it more difficult still. As did the white flag—a linen napkin—Paul picked up and started waving the minute he caught sight of her.

Coupled with his droll expression of chagrined repentance, Joy couldn't help but shake her head with an exasperated chuckle.

"Honestly," she said, moved to uncharacteristic shyness by the storm of feelings that assailed her. "You're too much."

"No." Every hint of playfulness left Paul's expression. He caught both of Joy's hands in his and pressed a soft kiss on the back of each.

"No, *carsya,*" he said quietly, "I am an insensitive boor."

"You are not." Joy tried to mask the surge of love she felt for him by feigning indignation. "And I'll bite anyone who says so."

As she had hoped, that made Paul smile. "The way you bit brother Ernie?"

Joy colored. "He was mean to you."

"And you couldn't allow that, could you?" Paul said softly. "My Good Samaritan."

Joy couldn't think of anything to say. She could only smile a tremulous smile and be warmed by the smile Paul returned before he kissed each of her hands once more and released them.

With a deep breath, his smile and demeanor took on an air of purpose. He stepped away from her and, with a flourish, indicated the table he had set, complete with a bouquet of red carnations.

"If madame would care to freshen up," he pronounced, exaggerating his British-flavored accent, "dinner will be served forthwith."

* * *

There was no awkwardness between them during the dinner of beef Stroganoff with pasta and fresh, steamed asparagus.

Though Paul seemed pensive and subdued during quiet moments, they chatted amicably of this and that, with Paul relating several small, humorous incidents about that afternoon's moving and storage of Joy's belongings.

Joy, with her second glass of Beaujolais, found the courage to ask Paul about coming along on the Cameron School field trip to Cannon Beach.

"Haystack Rock is a Cannon Beach landmark," she explained. "It's one of the many picturesque outcroppings of rocks—monuments to prehistoric earth movements and volcanic activity—that distinguish the Oregon coastline."

She went on to explain that, during low tides, the rock was a great place to get a look at marine fauna and flora in their natural habitat.

"Sounds fascinating." Paul was enthused. Apart from the fact that he genuinely enjoyed children, he liked nothing better than to share his love and knowledge of marine life.

They cleared the table and washed the dishes, working companionably side by side.

"Don't worry about putting away the stuff we moved here to the house," Paul said, very capably wielding a dishrag while Joy dried. "I've gone ahead and hung all the clothes in your closet—it was a bit of a squeeze, but should do for the moment. And I found places for the linens, as well. The dishes and other sundry odds and ends are in boxes on the back porch, well out of harm's way until you get time to go through them."

"Oh, good. Thank you." Joy heaved a sigh of relief. "I really wasn't looking forward to tackling any of that yet tonight."

"How about a short walk?" Paul suggested when the last pan had been stowed beneath the stove. "I could do with a breath of air."

But Joy begged off. "I'm for a hot shower and bed. You go ahead."

Instead of the shower, Joy opted for a relaxing soak in the tub. Humming to herself, she walked into the bathroom to turn on the taps and got quite a shock. Paul's toiletries and shaving kit were neatly arranged next to her things on the shelf by the sink and mirror. Some socks of his had been hung to dry over the towel rack next to his—also neatly folded—towel.

And on the peg on the back of the bathroom door, next to Joy's own long toweling robe, hung Paul's abbreviated kimono-style one.

Jiminy Cricket. Joy pressed a hand to her thundering heart. It's just as if—

"Everything okay?" Paul stuck his head through the open door with a perfunctory knock.

As usual when startled, Joy gave voice to the very thing she'd been thinking. "It's just as if we were married."

"Yes." The light left Paul's eyes. "I'll go for that walk now," he said. "Will you sit with me for a bit after your bath?"

"Sure," Joy said, troubled by his mood. "I'll hurry."

Paul had hot chocolate ready when Joy, who had settled for a shower, after all, and covered to her toes by her bulky bathrobe, padded barefoot into the living room only fifteen minutes later.

"You keep this up," she quipped, worriedly studying Paul's somber expression as she settled into one the overstuffed chairs, "and you'll make me want to keep you around forever."

"And wouldn't that be a fate worse than death," Paul replied in a likewise effort to lighting the atmosphere.

Momentarily flustered from having inadvertently trodden up a path left better unexplored, Joy gazed around the room.

"You've done wonders in here, Paul. Have I thanked you?"

"No thanks are needed, *carsya mu*. The chimney sweep did a lot more work than I."

"But still," Joy persisted, loath to have the subject end and chance a lull in their conversation. Silences between them had a way of... unnerving her. Of making her all too aware of the attraction he held for her. After the fiasco last night, it was something she'd really rather avoid. "I only did a very cursory tidy-up in here on Sunday, but now the room looks as good as new again."

Paul shrugged. "It gave me something to do. I'm glad you are pleased."

"I am. Really."

"I believe you, *carsya*." Paul's tone was threaded with amused exasperation. He knew exactly what Joy was trying to do, namely to avoid at all cost any kind of personal conversation.

Unfortunately, he knew only too well that they no longer had the time to indulge in the luxury of these evasive tactics. There were important things that needed to be said tonight.

"About last evening..." He set down his mug with a decisive *clunk*.

Joy reacted with predictable alarm. "Oh, please, let's not—"

"On the contrary." Leaning forward, Paul took Joy's empty mug out of her hands, too. It joined his on the small table between their chairs. "Let's. You mentioned Anna."

"Oh, hell." With a defeated sigh, Joy let her head drop back against the chair. "I don't want to talk about this."

Paul ignored that. "You said I called you by that name when I kissed you."

He reached for her hand.

Joy's head popped up, her expression wary.

"Don't do that," Paul chided. "I have no intention of pouncing on you."

"Sorry."

Paul made a short sound of dismissal and said, "Do you remember, *carsya*, what I told you that time you came to see me just before the wedding?"

"You said quite a number of things," Joy murmured. And remembering, some of them could still make her blush.

"Yes, but I especially recall saying that there would have to be honesty between us if we wanted to make the marriage work."

"And do you want to?"

"I have *always* wanted to," Paul said intently. "In your heart you know that. And speaking of hearts..."

He smiled. "In spite of the amnesia I suffered during part of our tumultuous acquaintance, I can recall with crystalline clarity every one of the kisses you and I have ever shared. And, believe me, I was aware of exactly *who* I was kissing every one of those times."

Paul's hand gripped Joy's more tightly. "It was you, Joy Marie. Every time. I know, because nobody's kisses have ever been as sweet."

As he spoke, Paul got up off his chair and, holding Joy's hand between both of his now, hunkered down in front of her chair.

Joy, helplessly trapped by the power of his unwavering gaze and by the gentle strength of his hands, felt the last of her carefully reerected defenses against him crumble into dust.

"Oh, Paul," she cried brokenly, putting her free hand over her eyes to shut out the intensity and pain. "Don't..."

"No, Joy." He removed her hand. "Honesty, remember? And so tell me, *malia mu,* when it was that you heard me call you Anna? Because I must have said her name, for how else would you know of her?"

Miserable, Joy averted her gaze and blinked back tears. "It was when I took you from here to my apartment," she said. "You were feverish, out of your head. I managed to get you out of the car. You weren't very steady, I had to hold you up. We stood very close on the sidewalk. You looked at me. I looked at you. And the next thing I knew—"

She bit her lip, letting the sentence hang. God, how vividly she remembered the heat and the need of that unexpected very first kiss.

She remembered because those feelings had stayed with her ever since. Worse, they had grown until they all but consumed her.

Joy turned her head and, unshed tears stinging her eyes, whispered, "Who is she, Paul?"

## Chapter Eleven

"**A**nna *was* my wife." Paul closed his eyes and tried to block out the flood of memories. "She is dead. They are both dead."

Paul's pain was a tangible thing. In the face of it Joy's moment of anguish—jealousy, really—seemed paltry. She longed to offer comfort, but Paul, still crouched before her and still holding her hands, seemed to have removed himself to another time and place.

"Both?" she whispered.

"Anna and Miguel." Joy had to strain to hear him. His eyes, open now, stared past her into space.

"Miguel." A boy? "He was your... son?"

Even through the haze of his remembered pain, Paul was so attuned to Joy, he perceived the distress that quivered in her voice. Giving his head a hard shake, he recalled himself.

His eyes focused on Joy's lambent ones and, managing a small smile of reassurance, he squeezed her arm.

"Come," he said. "Sit with me on the couch, where I can hold you."

Sensing Joy's hesitation, he softly added, "I really need to hold you right now, *malia mu.*"

How could she resist such a plea? Especially when her idea of heaven was to be in Paul's arms?

Joy let herself by guided toward the sofa and onto Paul's lap. But he didn't speak right away once they had settled themselves. With his chin resting on top of her head and his thumb sketching patterns on the back of her hand in a featherlike caress, he was content just to sit there and savor the closeness.

For quite a while Joy was, too. But then the need to know became too strong to deny. She drew back a little and looked into his face.

"Can you tell me about them?"

"They died." Paul watched his thumb smooth the back of Joy's hand and marveled that, suddenly, it no longer hurt to say those words. He wondered where the pain had gone. The pain that had followed him everywhere since that fateful day three years ago.

"Did it happen in a . . . fire?" Joy asked, and held on to his hand when he flinched and would have pulled away. "I wouldn't ask except, at one point when I was taking care of you, you were struggling, crying, 'Anna!' and, 'Fire! Fire!' You were so anguished, so desperate. . . ."

Joy kept a close watch on Paul's face. It had gone white, but was otherwise composed. That gave her the courage to ask, "Paul, was it . . . your fault? That they died?"

"No." It took Paul a while to utter the word that absolved him of blame. As recently as a year ago, he would not have been able to voice it.

"I was away. In my absence, Anna was entertaining...a friend—one of a string of...admirers. A candlelight affair. Very, ah, romantic. Or it might have been if one of the candles hadn't—"

Even still, bitterness choked him and he couldn't go on.

"If only I'd been there," he said when he could finally trust himself to speak. All the old guilts were rising from the ashes once more. "I might have been able to save Miguel at least. If only..."

*If only.*

Paul knew that his mentor would be tsk-tsking what he called Paul's penchant for martyrdom.

*We each forge our own destiny,* Dr. Lutti, his teacher, used to be fond of saying. *Only fools and egomaniacs fancy themselves able to forge it for others, as well. In your opinion, Commander, which one of the two are you?*

It had not been easy, but, in time, Paul had come to realize that he was neither, any more than he was God.

Now, taking a moment to remind himself of that, he felt the burden ease.

"Did you love her?" Joy asked in a small voice. "Very much?"

"Yes, I did," he said quietly. "In the beginning, before she taught me not to."

He bent his head and absently rubbed his cheek against Joy's hand, clasped in his. "But I adored her little boy. Miguel."

"He wasn't yours?"

"No. You see, Anna, too, was, uh, pregnant when I married her." Paul's voice, incredibly, was tinged with humor. "Although she, unlike you, did not see fit to inform me of this beforehand."

He stifled Joy's dismayed gasp with a kiss, chuckling. "You asked me, *carsya mu*. And yes, the similarities in our situations were not lost on me when you pulled that stunt on the Seacrest promenade."

"Oh, Paul..." Chagrined, Joy wished with all her heart they could *unlive* that awful episode by the police car. "How you must have despised me. And still you..."

"Yes," Paul said, dropping a kiss onto her nose. "And still I..."

He grinned. "Who says lightning doesn't strike the same tree twice, hmm? I may not be a tree, but I'm obviously a willing enough target. You figure it out."

Joy's meager smile gave way almost instantly to concern once again. "I can't believe you went along with my harebrained scheme."

"Your brother's fist in my mouth might have had something to do with it."

"He's crazy about you," Joy said, melting without thinking into Paul's arms when he urged her more closely into his embrace. "So's Ma."

"The feelings are mutual." Paul locked his eyes on Joy's. "I'm going to be sorry to leave them."

"Leave them?" Joy jerked back, stunned. "What're you talking about? What're you saying? Paul, what about... *us?*"

"Us?" Paul's eyes searched Joy's. "Are you saying you, too, want such a thing, *carsya*, hmm?"

Joy knew the time for coyness was past. "Yes."

"Ah, Joy." Paul pressed his face against her neck with a rough, shaky laugh. "I had despaired of ever hearing you say that."

Tremors shook him. Joy held him tight, moved beyond words by his reaction.

Paul struggled to get himself under control. "How happy I would have been to hear you say this even as late as yesterday."

His tone was laced with pain and regret. "But today? Ah, *carsya*..."

He glanced away. "Today it only makes me want to weep for every minute that we have wasted. Because, you see, it is too late for us, my Joy."

"Too late? Paul...?" Joy gripped his face and forced it back to hers. "What are telling me, that I blew it? That I—?"

"No, *malia*, not you. They."

"They?"

"I received a letter today. From the *INS*."

The way Paul emphasized the initials of the Immigration and Naturalization Service filled Joy with a terrible premonition.

"What?" Her voice sounded strange even to her own ears. Small, and forlorn. "T-tell me ..."

"Ah, *carsya*." Paul pressed her head to his chest, to his heart, and laid his cheek against her hair. "They regret—"

"No!" Wrenching away from him, Joy stared into Paul's bleak face with horrified incredulity. "No!"

His expression grim, Paul nodded. "It seems our neat little plan didn't work, *carsya mu*."

"But..." How could this be? What had they done wrong? Left undone? Overlooked?

"Oh, Paul." Joy's voice broke. "What're we going to do?"

Barely able to keep his feelings of helpless frustration in check, Paul mutely shook his head. He had asked himself that question all day long and had yet to come up with an answer. The hell of it was, he very much doubted there was anything more either one of them could do.

He looked at Joy, so pale and distraught, and their eyes clung in unhappy silence for long, torturous moments.

And then, suddenly, Joy came to life.

"Like *hell!*" she exclaimed, jumping off Paul's lap. Her expression dark, she furiously paced up and down in front of the sofa. "There is no way I'm going to let them do this. Nuh-uh. We're not going to take this lying down."

She stopped in front of Paul and glared down at him as if he were the culprit. "Dammit, Paul, I will not let them do this!"

Her eyes blazed with a zealot's fire. Crimson battle flags flew in her cheeks.

To Paul, she looked utterly invincible. Helen of Troy, Joan of Arc—Joy was all the legendary heroines rolled into one stubborn little package.

"My darling Good Samaritan," he said softly, loving her—as he had known he had loved her for probably as long as he'd known her. Her courage, her determination, her caring and, yes, her mulishness, too.

*"Malia eposa,"* he whispered, "darling wife, you tried. You fought the good fight. But now I'm afraid the time has come to concede."

"Never!" Appalled at the idea, enraged by Paul's seeming willingness to give up, Joy flung herself at him and gave him a hard shake. "I love you, dammit! Don't you dare talk to me of giving up!"

"What?" Paul gripped Joy's arms and held her still. "Say again what you just said."

Panting, Joy stared into the intensity of his eyes. "I said," she whispered hoarsely, "don't you dare talk of giving up." Hot tears now scalded her face.

Paul kissed them away. "No, *malia,* before that. What did you say before that?"

"I said..." Joy's chin fell to her chest with a desperate little sound.

"I said," she repeated slowly, "that I love you."

*"Trusora."* With a whoop of delight, Paul was on his feet, dragging Joy up with him and into his arms. He covered her face with kisses.

And then, his eyes ablaze with a fiery light, his lips captured Joy's in such scorching possession, all the fires that had been left to smolder in Joy since the previous night erupted into an inferno of need.

Without hesitation, with all the love in her heart, she responded to Paul's fervor. It seemed to her that everything, her entire life, had been one long journey toward this moment, when, at last, she would be one with this man. Her merman. Her husband.

Destiny had decreed it. Against all odds, he had been washed ashore on *her* beach, for her to find.

And having found him, nobody, not even the government of the United States, was going to take him away from her.

"I love you," she whispered, holding Paul, loving Paul. Needing Paul in the ultimate union.

Desperate to feel him, to know him, to taste him, her hands tunneled beneath his shirt, reveled in the feel of his skin.

Paul was hot, so hot. Burning up in a fever of need. Joy's hands on him were like tender instruments of torture.

"Stop," he murmured, struggling for sanity while he still could. *"Funato, malia,* this is madness," he whispered, even as his lips trailed across Joy's cheek, her jaw, the curve of her throat, which she arched to give him better access. "This is different. The letter. They will not let me stay. And I cannot protect you today. I don't have—"

"I don't care. We're married, and whatever happens, that's what I want. Please, Paul," Joy cried. "I'll need something to keep in my heart, if—"

"Shh." Paul kissed her, soothed her. Lord, he wanted her so much it hurt. And he, too, would need memories to cherish during the lonely times ahead. "Let's not think of it now. Of being apart. Let's not speak of it, not at all."

He held her close, stroking her, kissing her, murmuring foolish little love words as he nuzzled and tasted and touched and caressed. Joy's heart was drumming fast and hard, just as his own. It told him that she felt all the things he felt—heat, and want, and a need too strong to be denied.

"We're married," he whispered with awe. And he gloried in the freedom to touch her, taste her. To kiss her, again and again.

And Joy reciprocated in kind. She arched into him, offering him everything and desperate for more. "My husband," she whispered. "My darling. Oh, Paul, please..."

She caught his head in both her hands and forced him to look into her eyes. She infused the gaze she locked on his with every ounce of feeling she possessed, with everything that was in her heart.

*I love you.* She willed her eyes to tell him that, to make him see the emotion that was burning her up. And she longed with all her heart to hear him say those words to her in return.

"Love me, Paul, please love me."

Paul stared down at her. Joy's eyes were huge, wide and aware, and glittering with a desire that mirrored his own. But more than that, they were lambent with an emotion that transcended the physical.

Love. It was an emotion he had despaired of ever being able to inspire in those he—foolishly, it had seemed—cherished most. An emotion which, now that he saw it in Joy's eyes, both humbled and exalted him.

Nothing could have stopped him then from taking what Joy offered, and from giving in return everything he had it in him to give.

*"Trusora."* He kissed her, devoured her as the flames of passion, too long denied, devoured him. *"Malia mu,"* he murmured huskily. "My darling, *te ceriso... te adoro..."*

Joy's heart didn't need to know the language to understand the words Paul so fervently whispered as he kissed her, touched her, swung her up into his arms and walked with her into her bedroom.

With her own arms wound around his neck, Joy nuzzled Paul's cheek and throat, pleasantly abrasive in a wholly masculine way. She reveled in his scent, dipped the tip of her tongue into the hollow at the base of his throat where his pulse beat as erratically as her own.

She felt as fragile as spun glass, as treasured as a priceless figurine when he gently placed her in the middle of her bed. One of his knees came down on the bed next to her, and the mattress dipped as he braced himself and leaned over her. And just looked.

For long—and for Joy, breathless—moments he stayed that way and drank her in. His eyes, glowing like molten sapphires, moved across her face and torso with deliberate care. Each lingering pause was a thrill, the flaming intensity of his burning perusal like a physical touch. A tender caress. Never had Joy felt so desirable, never so desired.

"This is how I want to remember you," Paul whispered.

And Joy knew no shame beneath the blatant intimacy of his inspection and, now, his touch. Quite the contrary. Her confidence in herself as a woman grew a thousandfold beneath his impassioned regard.

She reached up and touched him. His face, his lips, the width and strength of his muscled shoulders. And then he was on her, around her, undressing her, touching her—all the things she was doing to him.

And *in* her, inside her. Joined with her. One with her. At last. At last.

"Mine," Paul murmured, driving deep and sending them both to the edge and beyond in a shattering disintegration of their separate selves. "*Eposa mu.* My wife. My wife. *Te ceriso....*"

They slept, closely entwined, exquisitely sated.

Sometime later—hours, minutes?—Joy awakened, slowly, as from a dream. For an instant she panicked—*had* it only been a dream?

But then she felt her husband's reassuring bulk against her back, the possessive weight of one arm and a leg anchoring her to his warmth.

She lay still, barely breathing, soaking in the happiness, the delirious knowledge that he was hers. Forever.

Until she remembered. The letter! The INS letter that threatened to take away this happiness before she had really even had a chance to savor it.

"Paul!" Suddenly frantic, she twisted around and shook him awake. It wasn't easy.

Confusion clouded his eyes as he sleepily stared up at her face. And then he smiled. A slow, sexy smile that curled Joy's toes.

"*Malia.* Come back to me." He drew her down to him. Nibbled at her lips. "What is it, *eposa?* Let me love you some more."

Oh, how Joy wanted to just give in. To just relax against him and enjoy all that should be theirs to enjoy for a lifetime.

But there was the rub. Unless they fought this thing, there would be no lifetime for them.

"Paul. No. We have to talk." Joy determinedly struggled out of Paul's rapidly more passionate embrace. "Paul. Listen to me. That INS letter, where is it? What, exactly, did it say?"

At her urgency, Paul at last came fully awake. His hold on her slackened, though he didn't release her completely. He scooted up against the headboard into a half-reclining position, settling Joy in the crook of his arm.

"What are you thinking?" he asked, inhaling the scent of her hair. It was the first thing about Joy he remembered. In his delirium, the scent of her had transported him back once again to the sun-filled meadows of his boyhood.

He dropped a kiss against her temple. "What's going on in that devious little mind of yours, hmm?"

"Nothing so devious." Joy drew away. She couldn't think when he nibbled on her like that. "This is the United States of America, where justice prevails. I'm simply going to demand some of that justice for us."

"That's all very well..." Paul stole a quick kiss and hungered for more. How would he ever be able to bear leaving her? Even if just for a while?

Because this he vowed, once deported—as he surely would be—he would fight heaven and earth to gain lawful entry into this country and to be reunited with his love. Even if it took every last *pharru* of his meager wealth.

"...if I were a citizen of this country," he pointed out. "But I am not and, therefore, I have no rights whatsoever under the law."

"Well, *I* have!" Joy declared with the light of battle blazing in her eyes. "And I, by damn, plan to exercise my rights. I'll appeal!"

"And I will do all I can to help you, *carsya mu*. But not tonight." Firmly, Paul drew Joy back into his arms and kissed the protest from her lips.

"Tonight is for loving, *malia*. And for making memories that will sustain us...."

*Ten days later*

"Ah. Mr. and Mrs. Mallik." INS Inspector Roy Mac-Millan was a large, balding man with a kind, grandfatherly face. At the moment, however, it was set in sternly professional lines. "Come in and have a seat. If you will."

He resumed his own seat behind a steel-gray utilitarian desk and flipped through a file.

*Their* file, Joy presumed. She was nervous—no, frightened was really more like it. This INS building, with its no-frills austerity, did not strike her as a place conducive to giving hope.

Her hand crept toward Paul's. It enveloped hers with warm strength and gave her the fortitude to settle more comfortably back in her chair as they waited for the inspector to speak.

He took his time. He thumbed through the file, stopping to read here and there, while every now and then glancing up at them with a frown.

"As you're aware," he finally said, "I have been assigned to make a judgment regarding your appeal. I was not the principal agent on this case. That was Agent Sommerville, wasn't it?"

"Yes," said Paul, while Joy only nodded.

"Did he treat you fairly, would you say?" MacMillan asked.

Paul inclined his head. "Oh, yes. He was courteous and professional at all times."

"All his findings and conclusions were correct?"

"I believe so, yes."

"You're not a political refugee?"

"No."

"You're not in any way oppressed, deprived or in need of sanctuary?"

"No."

"You agree with that assessment, Mrs. Mallik?"

"Uh, yes. As far as it goes."

"Which, I gather, since you are the one who instigated this appeal, in your opinion is not far enough. Am I correct in saying that, Mrs. Mallik?"

"Yes." More at ease, Joy nodded emphatically. "You're quite correct in saying that."

"I see." Leaning back in his chair, the inspector eyed Joy sharply over the top of his half-moon glasses. "Your appeal cites, uh, let me see—"

Tilting his head back, he scanned the page he held in his hand.

"Unusual circumstances that were not fully explored," Joy supplied.

"Yes..." MacMillan pursed his lips, his gaze once again on Joy. It shifted to Paul and then lingered for several heartbeats on their hands, still securely clasped and resting on Paul's thigh.

"I understand congratulations are in order," the inspector said, addressing Paul. "You were recently married. Rather sudden, wasn't it, Commander Mallik?"

"Oh, I don't know. Time is a relative thing, isn't it, Inspector?" Paul pressed Joy's hand and smiled into her eyes. "I mean, when you know someone's right for you, why wait?"

"Why, indeed?" MacMillan drawled silkily. "Especially if that 'someone' so conveniently happens to be an American citizen. Isn't that so, Commander?"

"No!" Outraged, Joy wrenched her hand out of Paul's to point the forefinger of it accusingly at MacMillan. "You're just as prejudiced about this as Sommerville was! But I'm here to tell you my citizenship had nothing to do with any of it! Paul didn't even want to marry me, for heaven's sake. He couldn't wait to get away from me, to get back to his ship. But I wouldn't let him. Do you hear me? I *made* him stay and marry me!"

Tears of frustration filled Joy's eyes, but she refused to back down or look away from MacMillan's pensive gaze.

"You *made* him marry you." MacMillan's brows arched as he shifted his eyes to Paul and looked him over. "Offhand, I'd say Commander Mallik's got about five inches and at least fifty pounds on you."

He paused a beat, pinning Joy again with his stare. "Which makes me wonder, Mrs. Mallik, just how you could *make* the commander do anything?"

"I have this big brother."

"I beg your pardon?"

"Nothing." Abashed, Joy waved her remark away. "A little humor..."

MacMillan's brows arched higher.

Joy cleared her throat. She was only too aware that this was it and that she'd better not blow it. She felt the heat of embarrassment burning her cheeks and willed it away.

"I made Paul marry me by telling him very loudly, in a public place and in front of witnesses, one of them a cop, that I was expecting a baby."

"And were you?" MacMillan blinked. "*Are* you, uh, in the family way, Mrs. Mallik?"

"No." Joy shook her head. "That is, I wasn't then. But now..."

Her gaze flew to Paul who was looking at her with an expression of such passionate possessiveness and pride, her throat closed up with emotion. "...I couldn't say for sure."

"I see." The inspector eyed her thoughtfully for long moments.

"Mrs. Mallik," he finally said, very quietly, "are you telling us you now could be? Uh, pregnant?"

If possible, Joy's cheeks flamed even more hotly than they had before.

Paul caught her hand again in his and the memories of their days and nights of lovemaking flowed hot and strong between them.

And Joy whispered, "Oh, yes," returning the pressure of Paul's hand. "I very definitely could be."

"Ahem." The noisy clearing of MacMillan's throat made Joy and Paul reluctantly, somewhat sheepishly, turn their attention back to him.

Looking relaxed and friendly for the first time since Joy and Paul had come, the inspector had tipped back his chair and folded his hands across his middle. "My wife and I have been married going on forty-two years now," he said.

"It was in Sacramento, I was on my way to a new assignment in L.A. and my car had broken down. Fuel pump, as I recall. Marsha—that's my wife—was on her way to visit an old school chum and was driving by the garage where I was having my problem taken care of when her tire went flat.

"We bumped into each other as she walked into the garage and I was leaving to grab a cup of coffee. We were married a week later so she could come with me to L.A. So you see, Commander, I agree with you."

MacMillan snapped forward, rocking his chair back onto all fours. "When you know something's right, why wait?"

Scooping the file off his desk, he stood.

A little uncertainly, still holding hands, Joy and Paul stood, too.

"I see a lot of people in this job," MacMillan said sternly. "And I hear a lot of stories. Some true, some not. Some move and convince me, some don't. Yours did.

"Commander Mallik—" Across the desk, he offered his hand.

Paul was quick to reach out and take it. They shook, a strong, hearty handshake.

"Welcome to the U.S., young man. Your temporary registration and work permit will be in the mail to you in a couple of days. Give us about six, eight months for the rest. Good luck to you, sir."

MacMillan turned to Joy with a grandfatherly smile. "And you, Mrs. Mallik..." He winked. "Knock 'em dead."

Out on the sidewalk, Paul exuberantly swept Joy up in his arms and spun her around.

"You did it," he shouted. "You incredible woman, you did it."

He kissed her—a short, hard, passionless kiss of happiness. And then he grabbed her hand. "Come on. This calls for a celebration. Where shall we go?"

"Home," Joy said, resisting when Paul tugged on her hand to move her along. "I want us to go home and make love."

*"Carsya."* Paul stood stock-still, all the laughter fleeing from his eyes to leave them dark, and fiercely intent. "What are you saying?"

"I told the inspector that I might be pregnant and I want to be darn sure I didn't tell him a lie. I love you, Paul Mallik." Joy's chin came up. "And if you love me back even a little bit—"

"What!" With a whoop, Paul scooped her up and whirled her around again and again. "Even a little bit?"

He set her down, his eyes blazing into Joy's. "My God, *trusora,* don't you know? Haven't you seen it, felt it? Haven't I told you—?"

"Not in English."

"I'm crazy about you," Paul said loudly. "How's that for English? Joy Marie Mallik, I'm madly, totally, irrevocably in love with you!"

And while Joy's head still reeled and her ears still rang with the love words she had so longed to hear, Paul demonstrated his love by kissing her with all the passion in his soul.

Above their heads, Inspector Roy MacMillan drew back from where he'd leaned out the window.

"Honeycutt," he informed his secretary with deep satisfaction, "that there young pair of lovebirds has what I'd call a very real marriage."

\* \* \* \* \*

She never dreamed she'd elope
at Thanksgiving....

Samantha Gray knew he was trouble the minute
she laid eyes on him. Not only did rancher
Logan Whitaker have a way with her fatherless kids,
he also made her feel like leaving her city widow days
behind. But she'd have to get past this rugged loner's
defenses before she could call herself

## LOGAN'S BRIDE
## (SE #995, November)
## by Christine Flynn

It's a

the season of lovinggets an added boost with a
wedding. Catch the holiday spirit and the bouquet!
Only from Silhouette Special Edition!

ELOPE1

## OFFICIAL RULES
## PRIZE SURPRISE SWEEPSTAKES 3448
### NO PURCHASE OR OBLIGATION NECESSARY

Three Harlequin Reader Service 1995 shipments will contain respectively, coupons for entry into three different prize drawings, one for a Panasonic 31" wide-screen TV, another for a 5-piece Wedgwood china service for eight and the third for a Sharp ViewCam camcorder. To enter any drawing using an Entry Coupon, simply complete and mail according to directions.

There is no obligation to continue using the Reader Service to enter and be eligible for any prize drawing. You may also enter any drawing by hand printing the words "Prize Surprise," your name and address on a 3"x5" card and the name of the prize you wish that entry to be considered for (i.e., Panasonic wide-screen TV, Wedgwood china or Sharp ViewCam). Send your 3"x5" entries via first-class mail (limit: one per envelope) to: Prize Surprise Sweepstakes 3448, c/o the prize you wish that entry to be considered for, P.O. Box 1315, Buffalo, NY 14269-1315, USA or P.O. Box 610, Fort Erie, Ontario L2A 5X3, Canada.

To be eligible for the Panasonic wide-screen TV, entries must be received by 6/30/95; for the Wedgwood china, 8/30/95; and for the Sharp ViewCam, 10/30/95.

Winners will be determined in random drawings conducted under the supervision of D.L. Blair, Inc., an independent judging organization whose decisions are final, from among all eligible entries received for that drawing. Approximate prize values are as follows: Panasonic wide-screen TV ($1,800); Wedgwood china ($840) and Sharp ViewCam ($2,000). Sweepstakes open to residents of the U.S. (except Puerto Rico) and Canada, 18 years of age or older. Employees and immediate family members of Harlequin Enterprises, Ltd., D.L. Blair, Inc., their affiliates, subsidiaries and all other agencies, entities and persons connected with the use, marketing or conduct of this sweepstakes are not eligible. Odds of winning a prize are dependent upon the number of eligible entries received for that drawing. Prize drawing and winner notification for each drawing will occur no later than 15 days after deadline for entry eligibility for that drawing. Limit: one prize to an individual, family or organization. All applicable laws and regulations apply. Sweepstakes offer void wherever prohibited by law. Any litigation within the province of Quebec respecting the conduct and awarding of the prizes in this sweepstakes must be submitted to the Regies des loteries et Courses du Quebec. In order to win a prize, residents of Canada will be required to correctly answer a time-limited arithmetical skill-testing question. Value of prizes are in U.S. currency.

Winners will be obligated to sign and return an Affidavit of Eligibility within 30 days of notification. In the event of noncompliance within this time period, prize may not be awarded. If any prize or prize notification is returned as undeliverable, that prize will not be awarded. By acceptance of a prize, winner consents to use of his/her name, photograph or other likeness for purposes of advertising, trade and promotion on behalf of Harlequin Enterprises, Ltd., without further compensation, unless prohibited by law.

For the names of prizewinners (available after 12/31/95), send a self-addressed, stamped envelope to: Prize Surprise Sweepstakes 3448 Winners, P.O. Box 4200, Blair, NE 68009.

RPZ KAL